HUMAN TRAFFIC

Detective Damien Drake

Book 5

Patrick Logan

Books by Patrick Logan

Detective Damien Drake

Book 1: Butterfly Kisses

Book 2: Cause of Death

Book 3: Download Murder

Book 4: Skeleton King

Book 5: Human Traffic

Chase Adams FBI Thrillers

Book 1: Frozen Stiff

Book 2: Shadow Suspect

Book 3: Drawing Dead

Book 4: Amber Alert

The Haunted Series

Book 1: Shallow Graves

Book 2: The Seventh Ward

Book 3: Seaforth Prison

Book 4: Scarsdale Crematorium

Book 5: Sacred Heard Orphanage

Book 6: Shores of the Marrow

First Edition: September 2020

Heav'n hath no rage like love to hatred turn'd, Nor Hell a fury, like a woman scorn'd.

- William Congreve

Prologue

"THERE ARE TWENTY-ONE baggies in front of each of you. You are to consume every one of these bags. Failure to consume all of the bags in the allotted time will result in you not getting on the boat. If you burst one of the bags, either on the table or in your mouth, you will not get on the boat. If one of these bags rupture inside you, you will die. Do you understand?"

The girl was blindfolded, but she could somehow sense that everyone around her was nodding. She did the same.

"Good," the man continued. "You have twenty minutes. That's one baggie per minute, give or take, so I suggest you get started."

The girl took a deep breath and then cautiously groped the table in front of her. When her hand fell on the first baggie, her heart started to race. It was much larger than she'd expected—about the size of a ping-pong ball, maybe even bigger.

Impossible... I won't be able to swallow one of these, let alone twenty-one.

And yet, when the man shouted that there were nineteen minutes left, she pinched the ball between thumb and forefinger and placed it in her mouth.

It tasted rubbery and salty, but she didn't let it rest on her tongue for long. With a heavy gulp, the girl swallowed.

The baggie only made it about an inch down her throat before triggering her gag reflex and she retched.

The baggie rolled back onto her tongue.

"I would like to remind you, that if *any* of the baggies break, you will not be getting on the boat."

The girl used two fingers to force the baggie down her throat. When she retched this time, she fought the visceral response by keeping her fingers in place. Her abdomen underwent a series of contractions, all designed to dislodge the bolus, but she persisted.

Eventually, her eyes bulged behind her blindfold and her body switched tactics. Desperate for air, instead of trying to regurgitate the baggie, she somehow managed to swallow it.

The girl could feel the thick wad stretch her esophagus all the way down to her empty stomach.

The second baggie went down easier, as did the third. By the last one, the twenty-first, the process had become second nature; it was as easy as swallowing raisins.

"Very good. I advise you to exercise caution as these bags will rub together in your stomach. If they burst, you will die. Now, stand up; one of my men will guide you to the boat."

Feeling queasy, the girl stood and someone immediately hooked an arm through hers.

"I'm trying!" someone to her left shouted. "I can do it! I just need more time!"

"Your twenty minutes are up," the man said in a flat tone.

There was a commotion, a struggle.

"I can—"

A single shot rang out and the room fell into silence.

"Get the baggies out of her," the man growled after the echo died down.

"How?" a second man asked.

"I don't give a shit how you do it—tear her open for all I care. Just get them out."

Trembling now, the girl bowed her head as she was led first down a dirt walk, then onto a floating dock. A few seconds later, she was vaguely aware of the fact that she'd boarded a vessel of some sort.

"You will be on this boat for nearly three days. During this time, you'll have access to a special drink, but no food. The drink tastes terrible, but it is important to consume as much as you can—this will help keep the bags from breaking. You can piss all you want, but it's in your best interest *not* to take a shit."

The grip on the girl's arm tightened and someone grumbled in her ear that they were heading down a set of stairs. The others were all around her now; she could smell the reek of their sweat, she could hear their shallow breaths.

When her bare toes eventually touched the landing, she was ushered across an empty space before being forced into a crowded room.

"After three days, you will be transferred to a shipping container for an additional day of travel. If, during this time, you defecate and lose one of the baggies, you will be left at sea. Now, as soon as I close this door, you can remove your blindfolds."

The girl was shaking now; the promise of a new life in a new land had suddenly lost all appeal.

This is a mistake, she thought. *I need to get out of here.*

But it was too late to turn back now.

She was not so naive as to think that the man's claim that they wouldn't get on the boat meant that she could simply go back to her previous life, as unappealing as the notion was.

Not getting on the boat really meant getting a bullet in the head.

Tear her open for all I care.

They weren't people anymore. They were simply a means of transportation—they were expendable, organic vessels containing something far more valuable than their lives.

"The next time you see the sun, you'll be standing on the shores of the greatest country in the world."

The pressure in the room suddenly changed as the door was slammed closed. This was quickly followed by a click that could only be one thing—a padlock being snapped shut.

With trembling hands, the girl reached up and lifted her blindfold.

Only she still couldn't see anything.

The room was bathed in darkness.

"Bon voyage," the man said from the other side of the door with a chuckle.

PART I

The Wrong Side of the Law

Chapter 1

DRAKE'S EYES SNAPPED OPEN and he sucked in a deep breath.

His initial instinct was to sit up, but he found himself unable. His muscles simply refused to obey his commands.

"Where—where am I?" he croaked. "Where the fuck am I?"

Blinking rapidly, the scene before him eventually started to become clear. Drake was in a small room of some sort, with annoyingly bright incandescent lighting embedded in the ceiling above. Off to one side, he noted an archaic-looking computer that beeped intermittently.

"He's back," a voice said, drawing Drake's attention. He turned his head in the direction of the voice, but this action sent his world into a tailspin and he was forced to close his eyes again. He retched and a thin fluid spilled from his mouth and coated his chin and cheeks. The vomit was sour and hot; just the idea of it brought more of it up from the pit of his stomach.

He was vaguely aware that someone was cleaning his mouth and face with a gloved hand. Confused, Drake opened his eyes again and found himself staring at the face of a man he'd never seen before. He was young with blond hair that was closely cropped to his head. There was a stethoscope dangling around his neck.

"Damien? Damien Drake?" The man asked, raising a penlight.

Drake squinted and tried to turn his face away from the offending light, but the man wouldn't let him. His gloved hand firmly gripped his chin as he waved the light back and forth. Drake tried to bring his right hand up to swat the man away, only he couldn't. And yet, unlike before, this was not the result of disobedient muscles.

Something sharp bit into his wrist, followed by the familiar sound of metal on metal when he relaxed.

He was handcuffed to the bed.

"Where am I?" Drake demanded.

"You're—" the man with a stethoscope didn't manage to complete the sentence; Drake was suddenly jostled, and for a split-second, he was airborne.

I'm not in a room, he realized. *I'm in the back of an ambulance.*

And the archaic computer to his left wasn't a Commodore 64, but a heart rate monitor.

Gritting his teeth against the nausea that returned with every bump, Drake pressed his brain into remembering what happened.

He recalled bits and pieces of his chase after Beckett's kidnappers, his journey to the farm. He also remembered speaking with someone... someone with dark hair and darker eyes.

Tears suddenly spilled down Drake's cheeks and he closed his eyes again.

I was too late... Beckett was already dead when I got there. And I should be, too.

"Is all this really necessary?" a new voice asked. Drake opened his eyes and looked around, trying to find the source, but he couldn't; the man was somewhere above his head.

"It's for his own safety," the paramedic said as he squeezed a clear IV bag.

"Bullshit," the second man replied. "It's because that douchebag inspector told you to cuff him. Don't lie to me. And if you keep squeezing a fucking bag like that, you're going to give him a goddamn emboli."

The voice was familiar, but Drake couldn't place it. The annoying ringing in his ears that was punctuated by the ping of the cardiopulmonary monitor on the rare occasion that his heart decided to pump was making it difficult to concentrate.

"I'm just doing—"

"Your job? Wow, that's a fucking new one. Why does everyone say that like it's an excuse for everything? *I'm just doing my job.* Oh, you know that SS soldier? You know the one... he killed millions of Jews because Hitler told him to—hell, he was just doing his job. What about the ISIS member? The one with the beard? Oh, he's a nice guy, really loves chess, long walks on the beach. It's just that Allah told him to blow up some Jesus lovers. And—" the man grunted in pain. "—shit, if you're so set on doing your job, why don't you give me something a little more powerful for my fucking finger? It hurts like a midget giving birth to triplets."

Beckett?

There was only one person he knew that spoke like this... but that man was dead. Wasn't he?

"Beckett," Drake croaked.

How is this possible? I saw Beckett's body on the ground with the disciples of the Church of Liberation.

A pale face suddenly hovered into view, and Drake had to blink several times to make sure that what he was seeing was actually there.

It *was* Beckett… the man looked tired, older, even, but there was no denying that smirk.

"What a fucking night, Drake. I mean, I had some doozies in the past—in college—but this one… this one definitely takes the cake."

Chapter 2

"Well, you gave your liver quite a jolt," the doctor with the round spectacles said. His demeanor was strangely jovial, given the circumstances. "And you very nearly died."

Drake grunted.

"No shit," he said. "But I've been training my liver for some time, now."

"I can see that," the doctor replied, still smiling. He held out a clipboard with some letters and numbers on it that Drake couldn't make sense of. The doctor shrugged. "You've got dangerously elevated liver enzymes, as well as other markers for fatty liver syndrome."

Drake didn't hear a question, so he refrained from answering.

"The good news is that your doctor friend there, Dr. Campbell, managed to get some hooch in you before you died from methanol poisoning. Normally, this would take hours, but it looks like you also consumed a high dose of Temazepam—sleeping pills."

Beckett suddenly appeared beside the doctor.

"Forced," Beckett corrected, sternly staring at the man with the clipboard. "Dr. Ramsey, he was *forced* to consume both the methanol and the sleeping pills."

Dr. Ramsey looked at Beckett with wide eyes behind his spectacles. Then he scribbled something down on the clipboard. Beckett tried to look over the man's shoulder, but he brought the paper to his chest like a student trying to avoid someone copying their answers.

Drake watched this with morbid fascination.

He wasn't sure if Beckett knew what really happened back at the farm and was just trying to save Drake's ass, or if he was just making assumptions. Either way, given the fact that he was still handcuffed to the gurney, Drake decided that it would be in his best interest to go along with his friend.

"Ray… Ray Reynolds forced me to drink it."

Dr. Ramsey's eyes turned to Drake. He had extremely thin eyebrows, which Drake found irritating, more so when they slowly inched up his forehead.

Drake wasn't sure what to say next, so again, he bit his tongue.

The doctor scribbled something on his paper again.

"Well, the good news is, I think you're going to make a full recovery. The bad news is that you're going to have to start making some lifestyle changes."

Drake frowned.

Why is it that doctors all use the same refrain—except for Beckett, of course, who punctuates his speech with f-bombs. Lifestyle changes…? What's with the euphemisms? Just tell me what you want me to do.

"I'll cut down on the alcohol," Drake offered pro-actively. He just wanted Dr. Ramsey gone now so that he could be alone with Beckett.

To find out what really happened back at the Reynolds's farm.

"And you're going to have to start exercising. You might only be 37 years old, but your body is that of a man twice your age," the doctor chuckled to himself. "Okay, maybe not twice your age, but at least fifty years old."

Drake couldn't argue with that—if anything, he felt compelled to correct the doctor's math.

He felt trapped in the body of a 100-year-old punch-drunk boxer.

"Sure, whatever." Drake raised his handcuffed arm. "Not going to run very far with these things on, though. When are you going to take the shackles off, doc?"

For the first time since entering the room, Dr. Ramsey's face sagged.

"I'm afraid that that's not part of my purview. You're gonna have to talk to the police about that."

Beckett clapped the man on the back, and he stumbled forward, nearly dropping the clipboard in the process.

"I think I'll take it from here. Maybe you should grab yourself a coffee."

Dr. Ramsey looked confused, but with further insistence, he eventually left the two of them alone.

"A good doctor," Beckett said after Ramsey was gone. "But my God, has he got some weird bedside manner."

"No kidding," Drake replied. He opened his mouth to add something else, but then closed it again. The truth was, he wasn't sure what to say. They had been through so much over the past few days that he figured anything he might come up with would either be inappropriate or insufficient. But the longer he thought about it, Drake realized there was only one thing he *could* say.

He cleared his throat.

"Thank you."

Beckett was never one for emotions, at least not for expressing them openly, and this was no exception. But Drake saw something in the man's eyes, something that confirmed that he wasn't just a heartless zombie. In his own way, Beckett cared.

"You're welcome, you asshole," Beckett said. Drake let his eyes drift to the man's left hand, which was wrapped in gauze.

"How's the finger?" Drake asked.

Beckett shrugged.

"How is it? Missing. But the only ones who care are my nose and my girlfriend, and I hate them both. If I'd been a surgeon… well, as ME, I don't have to worry about that. My patients are already dead."

Beckett strode forward as he spoke, and then started fiddling with Drake's handcuffs.

"What are you doing?" Drake asked.

Beckett grunted and then pulled the handcuffs away. Drake instinctively massaged his wrist.

"Getting you the fuck out of here, that's what," Beckett said, helping Drake sit up.

What the hell is going on?

"Oh, don't bother thanking me just yet," Beckett added sarcastically. "Thank your buddy Yasiv first. He's the one who gave me the keys."

Drake raised an eyebrow and waited for an additional explanation that never came.

"And Screech? Where's Screech?"

Beckett's brow knitted.

"He's fine… you really don't remember anything?"

Images flashed in Drake's mind, images of dead bodies and red plastic cups. Bits and pieces of Ray Reynolds's speech floated between his ears.

He shook his head.

"I remember… I remember leaving my office—that's it. The next thing I know, I'm waking up to your ugly face in the ambulance."

Beckett observed him for a good thirty seconds, trying to figure out if he was lying or not. Drake did his best to keep a straight face and must've done a satisfactory job because Beckett eventually nodded.

"Man, you got involved in some fucked up shit, you know that? Fucked up shit that cost me my finger and almost my life. If it weren't for Screech… and your brother, shit, if it weren't for them, we'd both be fucking our seventy-two virgins in heaven right now," he raised his gauze-covered hand and stared at it. "Come to think of it, that wouldn't have been that bad, especially with the shit drugs they're giving me for this pain. Seriously, I think someone replaced their supply of codeine with Mentos."

Beckett kept on rambling, but Drake had long since tuned the man out.

"My brother? Dane was there? Beckett, what the hell are you talking about?"

Chapter 3

SCREECH THREW THE TENNIS ball off the wall, and then caught it on the rebound.

"You serious? You really put all my money into Bitcoin?" he said into the headset as he tossed the ball again.

"Sure did," the man on the other line replied. "You said you didn't give a shit what I did with it."

Screech chewed the inside of his lip and squeezed the tennis ball as tightly as he could.

Fuck.

The vast majority of his money was from Bob Bumacher, the payout for 'returning' the man's yacht. And given what had happened on *B-yacht'ch,* what Beckett had done, Screech wanted to put some distance between him and the cash.

Still, he didn't want to lose it, at least not *all* of it…

Screech sighed.

"Well, that's that then. That shit crashed, man," he said. Although part of him felt the burden of the loss, another part—a larger part, he was pleased to realize—was bathed in relief.

The money just felt… dirty—*bitter,* even.

"Yeah, but here's the thing, Screech." The man paused and Screech stopped tossing the ball against the wall. He tapped the microphone to make sure it was still working.

"Alex? You still there? Hey, Banksy, you there?"

"*Uh-huh,* I'm still here. I was just pausing for effect."

Screech tossed the ball again.

"Well, okay, mission accomplished. What is it?"

"Well, let's just say I earned more than my ten percent management fee on this one. Screech, I turned your measly 75k into nearly half a million *ducats*."

Screech's eyes bulged and the ball rebounded off the wall and struck him in the side of the face.

"Fuck."

"A thank you might be more appropriate," Alex said with a chuckle.

"Are you fucking with me? A half a million?"

"Not fucking with you, my man. Got out just before it peaked. And that's half a mill *after* my fees—in a couple of months, no less. I mean, it can be a little less if you give me permission to treat myself to a nice bottle of Scotch…"

"Get yourself an entire case, Alex," Screech exclaimed. "This is unbelievable."

"Well, you better believe it. But now, we need to decide what to do next. My suggestion is to reinvest, because—"

Screech's heart was racing in his chest—he could barely contain his excitement. Seventy-five thousand was one thing, especially being dirty money, but half a million? Half a million could go a long way to appeasing anyone's conscience.

"No," he said. His throat was incredibly dry—so dry, that he had a problem getting the words out. "No, I should cash out."

"Come on, Screech. At least give me 100K to invest in something new. Maybe not cryptocurrency, but something else… real estate, maybe?"

Screech mulled his options. Turning 75k into 500 in just a few months—*Has it been that long already?*—was like winning the lottery. But Alex had done so well… and it was found money, after all.

He licked his lips, but they failed to moisten.

"I'll tell you what, reinvest a hundred grand… but the rest, I need the rest in cash, *babaaayyy.*"

Again, Alex chuckled.

"Sounds good, Screech. You want me to just cut you a check, or…" he let his sentence trail off.

Screech didn't know how to deal with 400k. Shit, he had no idea how to deal with seventy-five large. *Could* he get cash? And how large would a suitcase need to be to contain 400k?

With my luck, I'll get robbed on the way home from Alex's place.

"A check will be fine, Alex. I think—"

A sudden knock on the door drew Screech's attention.

It had been a while since Triple D had any visitors, ones that weren't the men in blue, that is. But he thought he was done with all that. He'd told them what he knew, what he'd seen at the farm.

He'd told them that he had no idea where Drake was, which was *mostly* true. But—

He shook his head.

No, stop feeling bad… you did nothing wrong, he scolded himself. *In fact, if it weren't for you, both Drake and Beckett might be dead.*

But there was a nagging voice in the back of his head that reminded him that if it weren't for him, maybe Ray Reynolds would still be alive.

You could have stopped Beckett; you could have saved Ray Reynolds and *Donnie DiMarco.*

And the pictures, Screech. You took the photos—

Another knock at the door pulled him out of his head.

"Hold on, I'm coming. Shit, don't bust down my door."

"What? What are you saying, Screech?"

Screech shook his head.

"No, not you, Alex. I'll call you back, I've got a customer," he said.

"All right, all right, I'll have that check made up for you, Screech. You swing by in the next couple of days, or I'll throw it in the mail. And don't worry about that 100k, cuz I'm gonna turn it into a cool million."

"Okay, sounds good, Alex. Talk soon," Screech said, clicking off the mic. There was a third knock, and he felt his anger rising.

These fucking cops…

Screech reached for the door and yanked it wide, a scowl on his face.

"I've already told you—"

The words caught in his throat.

It wasn't the police.

Instead, standing in the doorway of Triple D was a young girl who looked to be about seventeen years of age. She had dirty hair that hung in front of her face, and through those greasy strands, Screech could see that her cheeks were marred with tears.

"Shi—*shoot*, geez, I'm sorry. Are you… are you okay? Are you looking for somebody?" Screech stuttered.

The girl's shoulders slumped, and for a second, he thought that she hadn't heard him.

"Are you—"

The girl suddenly lifted her eyes and leveled the red lids at Screech.

"I'm looking for Damien," she said in a barely audible whisper. "I'm looking for Damien Drake."

Chapter 4

"**DRAKE... THAT WAS OVER** a week ago. I tried to reach your brother, but after the farm... I have no clue where he went."

Drake's eyes bulged.

"*A week*? I've been here for a fucking week? What are you talking about, Beckett? I was just in the ambulance... and then... and then..."

But Drake couldn't remember *and then*—he just saw flashes of meals being eaten, short trips to the bathroom, a parade of nurses and doctors. Sleep; there was that, too—lots of it.

His frustration bubbled over, and Drake yanked the IV out of his arm and swung his legs over the side of the bed. Another dizzy spell hit him then, but by gritting his teeth, he managed to stay focused. But when his feet hit the floor, his legs nearly buckled and he had to rely on Beckett for support.

"What the fuck is he even doing here?" he asked in a far-off voice.

"I've got no clue where he came from, Drake, or where he went. I only know that he came with Screech and if he hadn't... well, I think you know what would have happened to the both of us."

Drake's mind was swimming.

Screech... Screech who had taken the photos of him and Beckett and... *Jasmine?* Was that real, or just a nightmare?

Drake shook his head. It was a wasted effort trying to piece together the puzzle in his current state.

Even though his legs were weak from days of limited activity, Drake found that if he took his time, he could still manage to shuffle.

"Last time I spoke to Dane was eight or nine years ago, maybe even longer. He was backpacking through South America."

He bit back the urge to offer more. The truth was, the last time he'd seen his brother, *really* seen him, had been that day at the farm when he and their father had gone to pick him up.

In all of the intervening years, Drake had never been able to get out of Dane what had happened that week. All he knew was that it was something horrible. Something that had changed his brother forever.

And now he's back...

A flash of Raul and his thin mustache appeared in his mind.

Mr. Smith has a keen interest in your brother.

Did he come back for me, for Ray, or for Ken? Drake wondered as he searched the room for his clothes. He found them balled up on a chair, and he quickly slipped them on. They reeked of sweat and alcohol, which was becoming something of an unfortunate cologne for him as of late.

"Hey, Drake?" Beckett said. Drake turned to face his friend and was surprised to see that the man's face was pinched. "So, you know when I said that your buddy Sgt. Yasiv gave me the handcuff keys? Well, he may have given them to me, or I just might have borrowed them, if you catch my drift."

Beckett's eyes darted back and forth dramatically as he spoke.

Drake nodded.

"And that deputy inspector asshole Larry what's his name? Well, he wants to see you behind bars, my friend. Just giving you a heads up."

"No shit," Drake grumbled. "Thanks."

"Where are you going, anyway?"

Drake grabbed the door handle and spoke without turning.

"I've got work to do... I've got to find the Skeleton King."

Drake started to open the door then, but Beckett raced over and slammed it closed.

"What the fuck are you talking about?" he demanded.

Drake tried to pull the door again, but Beckett kept his hand on it.

"The Skeleton King... I've got to find him. I've got to put an end to this."

Beckett squinted at him for several seconds before answering.

"Drake... don't you remember?"

"Remember what? Beckett, I'm not in the mood for—"

"You caught him, Drake. You found the Skeleton King. It was Ray Reynolds, your brother's friend from childhood. He was the one leading the Church of Liberation, and he was the one responsible for killing all those people—including your partner, including Clay. You caught the guy. Well, I mean, if we're getting technical, I guess he kinda caught *himself*, so to speak."

Drake blinked several times as he tried to process what Beckett was saying. It sounded true... and Beckett's story jived with his broken memories, but—

The cups were scattered across the floor of the derelict farmhouse. Bodies were slumped against the walls, lying on the furniture, their eyes and mouths open. The smell of something astringent clung to the air.

His face suddenly went slack.

"No," Drake whispered. "He's still out there. The Skeleton King is still out there."

Beckett shook his head slowly.

"You caught him, Drake. He's dead. Maybe... maybe you should lie back down."

Drake's legs, which had regained some of their strength over the past few minutes, suddenly felt weak again.

And then his world started to spin.

Part of his mind, the ancient part that recognizes balance, noted that he was falling, but the message failed to stimulate any form of preventative action.

Before Drake realized what was happening, Beckett's arms were suddenly around him, without which he wouldn't be able to stand.

And then he felt something else, something equally as foreign as being held: there were tears on his cheeks.

"It's been... two years... this can't..."

Drake suddenly seemed incapable of forming a complete sentence.

...this can't be it, he wanted to say. *There has to be something more. The Skeleton King is still out there and I need to find him. I need to find him and make him pay for what he did to me, to Clay, to my brother, to Jasmine. To my* life. *I have to find him...*

Beckett suddenly pushed Drake away from him, but maintained his grip on his shoulders to prevent him from falling.

"I need to find him..." Drake finally managed. He raised his gaze and realized that Beckett was crying, too. In all of the time he'd known the man, Drake had never seen Beckett shed a single tear.

"Drake, I can't do this anymore, man. I mean, I've got my own shit going on, my own problems," as if to emphasize his point, Beckett held up his hand wrapped in gauze. "Good thing I'm not a fucking surgeon or my career would be over. And I found out in the Virgin Gorda that I'm not much for relaxing in the sun. The truth is, Drake… I gotta—I gotta take a break from you, from all this. Focus on myself for once."

Drake squinted at his friend. At first, he felt anger build inside him, but then he remembered the man saying something similar what felt like decades ago.

Everyone you try to help, everyone you ever try to help, ends up getting fucked in the end. And I'm not talking about the good kind of fucked, Drake. I'm talking about being flipped over and getting it in the ass with no lube. That *kind of fucked up.*

Drake swallowed hard and he wiped the tears from his cheeks.

"What do I do… what do I do now, Beckett?"

Beckett reached for the door, his face still sullen.

"I don't know, Drake. Maybe go see your pregnant girlfriend? That would probably be a good place to start."

Chapter 5

FOR SEVERAL MOMENTS, THE only thing Screech could do was stare. It was a painfully awkward situation, what with the teary-eyed girl looking up at him and Screech caught completely unawares.

"Is he here?" the girl asked in a soft voice. "Is Drake here?"

"N-n-no," Screech stammered. "He's not here—he's... he's out."

Several more awkward seconds of silence ensued before the girl bowed her head and started to turn. Screech almost let her go, but then he regained control of his faculties.

He reached for her arm, but when she recoiled from a simple touch, Screech withdrew his hand.

"Come in," he said, stepping off to one side. "I'm Drake's partner. I'm sure we can... I'm sure we can help you."

This was a lie, of course. After what had happened with the Skeleton King, and the whirlwind of death that Ray Reynolds had brought with him, Screech wasn't sure that there was anything he *or* Drake could do to help this girl. After all, the only reason that Drake had gotten his PI license was because there was one person left in the NYPD who didn't hate him and had helped expedite things. But after the farm... there was zero chance that it was still valid. As for Screech, he'd been hired as an analyst, and despite becoming part owner of Triple D and all of the shit he'd seen and done, he hadn't bothered to apply for a license himself.

He swallowed hard.

"Can I... can I get you something to drink?"

The girl walked into the room and looked around marveling at the surroundings. This was ironic, of course, given that their surroundings were anything but marvelous. In fact, they were one step above derelict.

"Water," she said at last. "Can I have a glass of water?"

As she spoke, Screech realized that she had an accent, one that he couldn't place.

Where the hell did you come from?

Shaking his head in confusion, he filled a cup with water and offered it to the girl. With shaking hands, she brought the cup to her lips. Then she drank; she drank as if she'd never seen water in her entire life. When she was done, the girl held the cup out to Screech and he promptly filled it again.

She only sipped it this time.

"Please," Screech said, waving an arm towards the row of chairs that were typically occupied by octogenarians. "Take a seat."

The girl nodded and continued to sip her water in silence.

Screech eyed her curiously. He had no idea what to do, what to say, or what to think.

But Drake… Drake would know what to do. There was little guarantee that it would be the *right* thing, but anything would be better than sitting here in silence.

"My name's Mandy," the girl said without looking up. "My name's Mandy and I need help. I need Drake's help."

Chapter 6

THE LIGHTS IN JASMINE CUTHBERT'S home were off and the driveway was empty. Drake hadn't seen movement from inside in the two hours that he'd been stationed in his rusted Crown Vic across the street. He had a key, of course, and provided that Jasmine hadn't changed the locks, he could go right on in. Only, he wasn't ready.

Drake couldn't imagine what the woman was going through. First, she lost her husband at the hands of a pedophile janitor, and then she'd fallen for his partner who was obsessed with finding his true killer. In the process, Jasmine had ended up pregnant. Just as things had started to take a turn for the better, just when Drake thought that their lives could improve, adopt some semblance of normalcy, he'd gone and dragged everyone back down again.

Ray Reynolds might have been a deranged serial killer, but he had also been right.

Right about a *lot* of things.

Drake brought the mickey of Johnny Walker Black to his lips and took a sip. It tasted familiar on his tongue, but when the liquid hit his stomach he felt a sharp jab of pain that he was unaccustomed to. Drake grit his teeth and dealt with his discomfort the only way he knew how.

He took another sip. And then another.

With trembling hands, he put the cap back on the bottle and stared out the window.

In the time it had taken him to find his Crown Vic and then make his way to Jasmine's house, more memories of what happened before he'd ended up at the Reynolds's farm came flooding back.

And with these memories, had come questions. *Unanswered* questions.

Beckett said that Drake had caught the King, that Ray Reynolds was the *true* Skeleton King. But while Ray Reynolds may have been the head of the Church of Liberation and he and his minions *called* themselves the Skeleton King, they weren't. They were Skeleton Princes, perhaps, or more likely just Pawns. But they weren't the King. Drake had been in this game long enough to know that there was always someone behind the scenes pushing the buttons.

Drake's hand started to ache and he was surprised to find that he was squeezing the plastic mickey so tightly that the top had started to bulge.

He took a deep breath and then placed the bottle on the passenger seat.

The King was still out there, and he had a name. His name was Ken Smith.

A set of headlights suddenly illuminated the dusk and Drake instinctively lowered himself into his car seat.

A black Volkswagen pulled into the driveway and idled for a few moments before the engine shut off.

And then Drake saw her and his breath caught in his throat. Jasmine was much bigger than he remembered; so big, in fact, that he considered that Beckett had lied to him, that he hadn't been out for a week in a coma or whatever the methanol had done to him, but maybe a month.

Jasmine was so big that walking was clearly an issue for her. Drake wanted to go to her then, to put his arm around the woman's waist and help her carry the groceries from the trunk to the porch. And he wanted to kiss her, too.

Most of all though, he just wanted to be normal.

In the end, Drake only sat in his car and watched.

He watched even as his vision blurred with tears, even after Jasmine had long since entered the house, even after he'd finished the entire mickey of Johnny Black, despite Dr. Ramsey's warning.

Drake didn't know how long he could wait there, but might have very well stayed rooted in place until his car was towed or he died—whichever came first.

But that was before the knock on his window.

Drake shouted in surprise and instinctively reached for the gun that had been sitting on his lap.

But when he turned, he didn't see a masked vigilante or even a local hoodlum. No, he saw the familiar face of a young woman.

With a painful swallow, Drake rolled down his window.

"What?" Suzan Cuthbert snapped. "Are you going to shoot me now? You pretty much killed my mom already… are you just back to finish off the rest of the family?"

Chapter 7

SCREECH RUBBED HIS EYES, but when he pulled his hands away, Mandy was still sitting across from him. The tale that the girl had woven was so horrific, so disturbing, so frankly unbelievable, that Screech wasn't sure that it hadn't been him who'd consumed the methanol and was having a hallucination on his way to the afterlife.

"And… and how did you hear about Drake again?" he asked, reaching into the top drawer of Drake's desk and pulling out a bottle of Johnny Walker Black. He wasn't accustomed to drinking during the day—in fact, he'd barely touched the stuff ever since returning from the Virgin Gorda—but it suddenly felt appropriate.

He poured himself a glass and was about to offer one to Mandy, before hesitating. When she'd arrived at the door, he'd pegged her as seventeen. When she told her story, Screech thought that she might be in her mid-thirties. Now, as she leveled her raw eyes at him, she could have been nine.

Screech decided to keep the booze to himself unless she asked for it.

"When I was in the shipping crate, right before I managed to escape, I heard them talking—"

"The one with the thick Spanish accent, that one?" Screech asked.

Mandy nodded.

"He was talking to someone—a Russian, maybe—and I heard him mention Damien Drake's name."

Screech took another sip of Scotch and mulled this over. While he had no reason to doubt the rest of the girl's story, this part wasn't sitting right with him. If Mandy had simply overheard Drake's name, and if this happened just a few days ago, then how the hell did she find Triple D so quickly? Hell, there must be hundreds of Drakes living in Manhattan alone.

"And what did these men say about Drake?"

Mandy hesitated before answering.

"They said... they said..." her sentence trailed off into nothingness.

Screech watched Mandy's face closely, wondering if he should either press harder or stop questioning her altogether. If he should fire off a second text to Drake or just give in and call the cops.

He took a mouthful of Scotch.

"It's okay if you want to stop. Are you hungry? Do you want to go somewhere to eat? I can buy you dinner," Screech cringed at his own words. He sounded like he was asking Mandy on a date. "What I mean is, we can go eat if you want, if you're hungry. Or if you want to use the phone... is there someone in Colombia that you want to call? Or do you want me to get the police over here?"

When Mandy spoke again, it was clear that she hadn't been paying attention to his ramblings.

"They said that Drake was making things hard for them, something about how he was getting closer to figuring out what was really going on." She paused to catch her breath, and Screech became acutely aware of just how frail she actually was. It didn't look as if Mandy had eaten in days. "They said that he was going to catch the King...? *Rey Esqueleto*?"

The glass of Scotch almost slipped from Screech's hand. He was gaping now, but couldn't help it.

His Spanish was rudimentary at best but he was fairly certain that *Rey Esqueleto* meant Skeleton King.

Why the hell would people packing drug mules from Colombia in shipping containers know about the Skeleton King?

Screech tightened his grip on the glass and finished what was left.

"Is there anything... anything else you can remember?"

Mandy lowered her eyes again and shook her head.

"It was dark... they gave us this stuff to drink, said it was important. It tasted horrible, like so bitter. But I drank it. The other girls... I think they might have been drinking sea water and that made them sick. And they started... they started to *scream*. And then, after a while, it was quiet. Then it was only me."

Thinking that Mandy was going to burst into tears again, Screech stood and walked over to her. He laid a comforting hand on the girl's back, but when she shied away from his touch, he pulled away.

"Sorry," he grumbled. And then he just stood there for the better part of a minute staring off into space

Screech didn't know what to do, but he knew he had to do *something*. He took his cell phone out of his pocket and dialed Drake's number, silently pleading for the man to pick up.

It went directly to voicemail.

After grumbling a curse, he finally made a decision. He wasn't going to the police. That idea had been shot down the second Mandy had mentioned the Skeleton King. There were just too many connections between Deputy Inspector Palmer and ANGUIS Holdings and the Church of Liberation and Ray Reynolds and Ken Smith and Raul and Dane Drake and —

Screech bit the inside of his cheek so hard that he drew blood.

"Come on," he said at last. "Let's get you cleaned up and see if we can get you something to eat. By then, Drake'll be around to help."

If he's still alive, that is.

Chapter 8

DRAKE WAS SO STARTLED by Suzan's presence that he almost failed to react.

"So?" she demanded. "Are you going to shoot me or not? Because if you aren't, I suggest you get out of the car and come inside. Oh, and leave your gun on the seat just in case I decide to use it on you, instead."

Drake, still in a daze, opened the door and stepped out of the car.

Once outside, Suzan did the unthinkable. She reared back and slapped him. The blow was hard enough to cause Drake's eyes to water and his cheek to sting, but wasn't hard enough to do any real damage.

And then Suzan proceeded to do the second most unexpected thing: she leaned forward and hugged Drake tightly around the waist. As she did, she whispered, "You're a fucking asshole, you know that? But as much as it pains me to say this, I'm glad you're okay."

Drake, still confused and a little buzzed, hugged her back.

"I… I don't know what to say," he managed at last. Suzan pulled away and guided him towards the house. Drake was apprehensive of seeing Jasmine—*everyone you try to help, everyone you ever try to help, ends up getting fucked in the end*—but judging by what had just happened, he doubted his ability to weasel his way out of it.

And if he did, it wouldn't surprise him if Suzan actually grabbed his gun and shot him.

"Well, you better figure it out quick, Drake. Because Jasmine's going to have a lot of questions."

***

All three of them were sitting at the kitchen table with tears in their eyes. Jasmine's reaction had been much like Suzan's, minus the slap, of course. She'd been overjoyed with the fact that Drake was okay, that he wasn't hurt, but she was also confused.

"I don't understand... I called all the hospitals, Drake—*all* of them. And you weren't registered."

Drake took a sip of his scalding black coffee and wished he hadn't sucked back the entire bottle of Johnny in the car. His head was still foggy, and his guts roiled something fierce.

"I was there. I was in—" his eyes fell on the hospital bracelet that was wrapped around his wrist. "See? I still have the bracelet."

But as Drake turned the bracelet, he realized why neither Jasmine nor Suzan had been able to find him. While the typed name had his initials, instead of reading Damien Drake, the bracelet read Dirk Diggler. Beckett must have changed his name to keep DI Palmer and his goons away.

"I was under a different name," he said, but this explanation did little to clear up the confusion.

"But why, Drake? I don't understand. One minute you're sitting here beside me watching TV and the next you're up and gone. I don't hear from you, I can't get a hold of you, none of your friends answer their phones. Two weeks later you show up looking like hell, saying you had been in the hospital under a different name. And then there's all the stuff on the TV, the news about the Skeleton King. About... Oh God, Drake, they're talking about Clay again."

Drake bit his lip in frustration. He'd wanted to keep Jasmine out of this. Even though he had been certain that Peter Kellington wasn't the man responsible for killing her husband, and this had proven to be the case, the last thing Drake wanted was to drag her back into this. To grieve a second time for the same person was a horrible thing. And yet, that's exactly what had happened.

"Is this all connected?" Suzan demanded. "And you better tell me the truth, because I swear to God I'll just go to Dr. Campbell and you know he'll tell me everything. So, for once in your life, Drake, just tell us the goddamn truth."

Drake sighed and lowered his eyes to the coffee cup clutched in his hands.

He couldn't tell them the truth, could he?

Drake swallowed hard and then began speaking.

Chapter 9

SCREECH TOOK MANDY TO his apartment. It wasn't his first choice, but just sitting in the car beside her for a few minutes was enough to curdle his stomach.

She desperately needed a shower.

He politely led her to the bathroom and then made sure to tell her several times that he would be on the couch not twenty paces away. He even went as far as to say that he wouldn't move, unless she wanted him for anything. Screech regretted saying that last part. In fact, every time he opened his mouth he sounded like some sick pervert just trying to get in her pants. Speaking of which, the only thing that he had to offer her was a pair of sweatpants with a tight drawstring and a plain white T-shirt.

"We can get you real clothes from the store later… for now, it's just something clean to put on."

Mandy nodded at this and then retreated to the bathroom.

Screech grabbed a beer and plopped down in front of the TV. He had just changed to the news when he heard a strange series of sounds from the bathroom. It was hard to hear clearly with the shower running, but it sounded like Mandy was gagging.

He opened his mouth to ask if she was okay, but knew that something stupid would come out—*are you gagging? I can help you with that. I was a lifeguard in middle school*—and decided against it. The sound lasted only a minute or so before he heard the shower curtain being pulled back.

"What the fuck is wrong with you?" he asked himself. "Just be normal."

As luck would have it, he'd arrived just in time for the 9 o'clock news report, which just happened to be about the

Skeleton King. Screech turned up the volume and watched as a blond talking head stared awkwardly into the camera without blinking.

He was half-convinced that she was a robot.

"I'm joined by NYPD Deputy Inspector Lewis Palmer who headed the investigation into the horrible tragedy at the farm just outside the city. Inspector Palmer, how did you first find out about this Church of Liberation?"

The camera panned to DI Palmer and Screech felt his upper lip curl. The man looked as smug as ever.

Heading the investigation? You didn't want anything to do with it, you prick. It was Drake who did everything.

"Please, Josie, just call me Lewis. We first had an inclination that there was something sinister going on when we found the body of one of our own, NYPD Detective Simmons, who had been brutally slain. I immediately went to the mayor and asked for his full support, and he was very gracious in giving it. From there, we managed to trace the detective's movements shortly before his death. And this led us to a specific religious group called the Church of Liberation, as you mentioned. After some very strong detective work by our men in blue, we were eventually led to a long-deserted farm. There, we found more than a dozen members of the church, along with its leader, a Mr. Ray Reynolds, all of whom were deceased."

Inspector Lewis was smiling as he spoke and Screech's lip curl became a scowl.

It was all bullshit, of course. All of it, every last word.

Except for the dead. Screech had seen them with his own eyes.

"Lewis, can you tell us a little bit more about Ray Reynolds? And maybe address the rumors that Ray Reynolds

and the church was behind the Skeleton
took place over a year ago in New York
When the camera panned back to ins
was gone.

"As the investigation is ongoing, the
details that I can reveal at this time. At
that these are isolated incidents and not
previous crimes, aside from Detective Si
for Ray Reynolds, we know that he grew
his family owned the farm in which we f
congregants. We know also that Ryan Re
orphan at fourteen, but we're not sure w
in the intervening period prior to starting
Chapter of the Church of Liberation roug
As I said, Josie, the investigation is ongoi

Josie was looking down at her notes n
the camera was on her. Eventually, her u
popped up.

"And what can you tell us about this
that Ray Reynolds had a relationship wit
Smith... that the Church of Liberation ma
donation to Ken Smith's campaign last fa

Lewis looked as uncomfortable as a m
parents mid-coitus.

"I can assure you, Josie, that Mayor Sr
Ray Reynolds personally or have any int
Church of Liberation. As you know, liter
association can make a donation to a cam
Mayor Ken Smith, for instance, had more
individual donors or groups fund his ca
responsible for, nor required to investiga
of those donating parties. As you can ima

nings on the go, including keeping New
cking down dangerous people like Ray

'almer offered after this little soliloquy
'd neglected to bury its own poop.
e'll find out more as this investigation
ıst one more thing before we go: there are
members of the Church of Liberation were
back. In fact, I'm getting a report that one
ex-NYPD officer, was not present. Can you
ports?"
e kidding me," Screech hissed as he
line of questioning was headed. "They're
him? *Really*?"
a eventually focused in on DI Palmer's face
hat that was exactly what they were going

ve are certain that there is no longer any
there is one particular person that we are
ing. His name is Damien Drake—I believe
creen? Ah, yes, there it is. While we don't
ous, he is a person of interest. If anybody
know someone who has been in contact
the number on the screen now."
his feet and threw the half-empty beer
His aim was off and it smashed against
ss shards and foamy beer to the carpet.
he screamed. "That's bullshit! You—"
A female voice asked.
round so fast that he nearly stumbled.
andy! What are you doing?"

Chapter 10

"SO, THAT'S WHAT HAPPENED," Drake said, still staring into his coffee. When there was no reply for several seconds, he finally looked up.

Jasmine was crying, which was what he expected, but he was surprised that Suzan was crying as well.

"What are you trying to say, Drake?" Suzan snapped, wiping tears from her eyes. "Are you trying to tell us that Clay was somehow involved with these people? With this fucking cult?"

"Suzan…" Jasmine interrupted.

"No, mom, I'm not going to be quiet, not again. I was quiet the whole time after dad died because I didn't want to upset anybody. But here's the thing, mom. I'm upset too, and have a right to know what really happened."

A photograph suddenly flashed in front of Drake's eyes.

A brick… Jasmine smiling, holding a brick of heroin… the same brick that Clay had confiscated from some addict…

He swallowed hard.

Did I really see that? Did Raul really show me that photo or did I imagine it?

His brain still hadn't fully recovered from the thrashing he'd given it, and he couldn't be sure… and yet, the way Jasmine just did a one-eighty, going from crying to chastising made Drake wonder.

Did she know more than she was letting on?

He cleared his throat.

What did it matter, now?

"Suzan, you've got it all wrong," Drake lied. "I don't think Clay was involved with these people at all. I think… well, I know this is going to sound bad, but I think that your dad was just at the wrong place at the wrong time. I think that night in the rain we were just getting too close to the Skeleton King and the Church of Liberation. I think that's why they killed him. If he'd just had a better partner… fuck… I just… I just wish it were me." Tears spilled down his cheeks, and Drake was helpless to hold them back now. "If it had been me instead of your dad, things would have been different. They *should've* been—"

"Don't say that," Jasmine whispered.

Drake ignored her.

"If it had been me that Kellington had shot and killed, imagine the pain and suffering that would never have happened to you guys, to everyone."

"Don't say that," Jasmine repeated a little louder this time.

"If I'd just done my fucking job properly and watched Clay's back, none of this had to happen—neither of us had to die. But if anybody deserved it, it was me."

Jasmine suddenly leaped to her feet.

"Don't say that! Don't you say that!"

Suzan, alarmed by her mother's sudden outburst, which was very much unlike her, went to Jasmine's side and laid a hand on her shoulder.

"Mom, please, calm down. You shouldn't get this upset."

Jasmine turned to Suzan then with tears in her eyes.

"Why shouldn't I get upset? I've already lost one man I loved and I can see it in your eyes, Drake, I'm about to lose another."

Drake was floored. Jasmine loved him. *Him.*

Why?

"We caught them, Jasmine. We caught the bastards who are responsible for Clay's death. Peter Kellington might've pulled the trigger that day, but it was this Church of

Liberation that was behind it all. And they are no longer. The man," Drake closed his eyes for a moment, and an image of his brother's friend, of Ray Reynolds with the red plastic cup in his hand, flashed in his mind, "who ran the church... he's dead now."

Suzan glared at him.

"Is that supposed to make us happy, Drake? Am I supposed to be happy that someone else had to die in this whole mess?"

This response was as unexpected as Jasmine's.

Was it supposed to make them happy? Drake had spent the better part of two years searching for the person truly responsible for what had happened to his partner and best friend. But after Ray Reynolds had died, Drake didn't feel any better. If anything, he felt worse.

It's because the real Skeleton King is still out there. Ken Smith and the other ANGUIS Holdings owners, whoever the fuck they are, they're the ones who are really responsible. Ray Reynolds was just a stagehand, a tool that could be shaped and molded to do Ken's bidding.

Drake shook his head.

"I don't know, Suzan. I don't know if it's supposed to make us feel better or worse or indifferent. All I know is that it happened."

Silence fell over them then, one that seemed to stretch out for an eternity.

It was eventually interrupted by Drake's cell phone buzzing in his pocket. It had been the fourth or fifth time since he'd arrived at Jasmine's house that it had rung. All those other times, he'd simply ignored it. Now, however, it was a welcomed distraction.

"I'm sorry," he said, pulling his cell phone out of his pocket. "But I have to take this."

When no one protested, Drake looked down at his phone.

It was Screech.

He stood and politely moved away from the table.

"Yeah?" he asked. "Not really the best time, Screech. What do you need?"

Drake had expected that this was something accounting-related or perhaps about a new Triple D job. But when he heard the desperation in Screech's voice, he knew that this wasn't the case.

This was something serious.

"What do I *need*? I *need* you, Drake? Things are all fucked up and I need to see you. I need to see you, now."

Chapter 11

"WH-WH—WHAT ARE YOU DOING?" Screech stammered.

Mandy stood before him, completely nude. Her long blond hair, now wet, hung past her shoulders, parting around small, perky breasts. There was a small tuft of matching blond hair between her legs.

"You saved me," Mandy said. She took a step forward, and Screech, unable to take his eyes off her, stepped backward.

"You should put some clothes on," Screech said. "Please, put some clothes on."

Mandy's eyebrows knitted.

"You don't find me attractive?"

Screech's eyes wandered up and down the woman's body; this wasn't planned, but he had little say in the matter. It was simply natural.

He swallowed hard.

"You are very attractive," he said under his breath. "But you are too young… too young for me."

Screech wasn't sure why he said this last part, but he chalked it up to being shell-shocked by what was going on.

Mandy shook her head.

"I'm twenty-four," she admitted with a smirk. "Is that too young?"

Screech shook his head.

"Please, just put some clothes on. *Please.* This isn't… isn't right."

When Mandy didn't move, Screech grabbed a blanket off the couch and gently wrapped it around her.

"My boss told me that men in New York like young women. I can be sixteen if you want. Fifteen?"

Boss... More like pimp, Screech thought as he guided her toward the bathroom. *Fifteen? Seriously?*

"No, no definitely not. It's just—" Screech wasn't sure how to continue. If Mandy really was twenty-four, that put her only two years younger than him. And she was literally throwing herself at him.

But she's also damaged and scared. And been through hell.

"Please, put on some clothes," he said for what felt like the hundredth time. "Drake will be here soon."

Mandy's coquettish demeanor suddenly changed.

"He's coming? Drake's really coming?"

Screech recalled the man's furious tone over the phone.

"Oh, he's coming all right."

***

Drake burst through the door to Screech's his apartment.

"Screech! *Screech*! Where the hell are you?"

Screech appeared from around the corner, eyes wide.

"Oh, fuck, thank god you made it. But now I think we should go, talk somewhere else—I don't think it's safe at my place. They're bound to be looking for you here, at the office, at Jasmine's house."

Drake was still trying to wrap his head around what Screech had told him over the phone.

He was wanted for questioning? By that asshole Palmer? And the man had put his face all over the news?

Drake wanted nothing to do with the DI, unless it was to punch him in the face.

He closed his eyes for a second, recalling the pained expressions on both Jasmine and Suzan's face when he told them that he had to leave again. They couldn't believe it, and Suzan for once wasn't shy letting her feelings be known.

But there was also the matter of the girl, the one who had come looking for him. The one who knew about the Skeleton King.

"Where's the girl?" Drake demanded, his eyes darting around the room.

"Drake, we gotta get out of here—"

"I asked you where the girl is."

Screech pressed his lips together and tilted his head toward a door on his left.

Drake strode past Screech, took one deep breath, and then opened the door.

A girl was seated with her back to him wearing a pair of track pants that were slightly too large and a T-shirt that was slightly too small. She was running a comb through her long blond hair and didn't appear to have noticed the door opening.

Drake hesitated and then announced his presence.

The girl turned, a smile on her face. She was pretty, with smallish features and bright green eyes.

"My name's Drake," he said. "My partner said you were looking for me?"

The woman nodded and leveled her eyes at Drake's.

"They're scared of you, Drake, which means that I think you can help. I think you can help me find the *pendejos* who killed my friends."

Chapter 12

"**WHAT DO YOU THINK** you're doing?" Sgt. Henry Yasiv demanded as he stormed into the Deputy Inspector's office. "Really? You're really going to go ahead and put Damien Drake's face on the news without even a discussion?"

DI Palmer took his time shuffling the papers in his hands before placing them on the desk and finally raising his eyes. He had slicked black hair and hawkish features, and while his appearance generally annoyed Yasiv, it was his voice that was most grating. It was slow and monotone, suggesting that everything he encountered in life was an incredible bore.

"Sgt. Yasiv, there was a discussion," the man said flatly.

With who? Yasiv almost blurted, but stopped himself just in time. That's what the man wanted. He wanted Yasiv to question him so he could pull the 'above your pay grade' card.

When Mayor Smith had first suggested that DI Palmer could help with Detective Simmons's case, Yasiv had been grateful. After all, it was his first high-profile case after taking the job as sergeant. But after that case had been closed, it became obvious that DI Palmer had another initiative—and that he wasn't leaving anytime soon.

Things had come to a head when Yasiv strongly suggested that they just let Drake walk, forget that he was even at the Reynolds's farm. After all, everyone in the Church of Liberation was dead. But Palmer was having none of it. In fact, he had wanted to ride in the ambulance with Drake. Shit, if Palmer found out that Yasiv had conveniently left his keys out in the open, right in front of Dr. Campbell, he would flip his lid.

"You can't just put a person's picture on TV, least of all one of our own. And especially not when Drake hasn't been charged with anything."

Palmer licked his lips before speaking.

"*Yet*. Sgt. Yasiv, might I take a moment to remind you of your rank? You may be the sergeant of 62nd precinct, but I am the Commanding Officer of Major Case Squad. I'm leading this investigation, and I recommend that you watch your tone moving forward."

Yasiv chewed his lip. Even though he was not a man prone to violence, Yasiv was positive that if things continued along these lines, it wouldn't be words that either of them would have to watch, but fists.

"You may be my superior, but it's customary to consult with the person in charge of a case before going on live TV. And the Skeleton King and Church of Liberation case? That was my case."

DI Palmer cocked his head to one side.

"You're right, Sgt. Yasiv. You're right that the Simmons murder and the Skeleton King cases were yours. And I let you take the lead on them. But those are now closed—you said so yourself. I'm pursuing something new now."

Yasiv's eyes narrowed.

"What case? And how is Drake involved?"

Again, a deliberate and annoying pause.

"I'm sorry, Sgt. Yasiv, but the details of this case are confidential."

Yasiv took an aggressive step forward, but Palmer didn't even flinch.

"Confidential? You're sitting here in my precinct in an office that I lent you... and now you're going to sit there and tell me that there's some bullshit case against Drake that's confidential?"

Palmer shrugged.

"*I* didn't mention Drake, *you* did. Sorry, but this comes directly from the chain of command and it stops at the DI. I'm more than willing to give up this office, but I'll have no choice to put that in my report for when I meet with the mayor later this month. So? Do you want me to leave?"

"You can keep the damn office," Yasiv snarled. "But I'm going above your head, Palmer. I'm going to find out what this personal vendetta that you have with Drake is all about. He's a good man, a great cop, and I consider him a friend. This isn't over."

With that, Yasiv spun and started towards the door. He was nearly in the hallway when Palmer managed to get the last word in.

"You know what they say about the company we keep, Sgt. Yasiv. A rising tide may float all boats, but when you don't have a boat, you're bound to get stuck in the mud. You'd do well to keep that in mind."

Chapter 13

DRAKE SIGHED AND RUBBED his palms together. Mandy's story had been horrible, but the sad fact was that he'd heard dozens of similar ones before during his time in the NYPD.

"So, when everyone else started collapsing, you did the same? Pretended that you were dead like them? And then you managed to sneak away after they opened the container? Do I have that right?"

Mandy nodded.

"Mandy, do you think that any of the other girls did the same as you? Pretended to be dead?"

The girl turned her head to the side and Drake saw her shudder.

"No. They were all dead," she replied quietly.

"And what did they tell you back in Colombia, exactly?"

As Mandy collected herself, Drake turned to Screech and asked him to fetch them a drink.

"They said that... that we would have a better life in America. That we could continue doing what we were doing in Colombia, but that it would be safe. That we would be protected."

Drake nodded. This was another common refrain of sex traffickers overseas. And, in all honesty, it was usually true. The risk of being murdered while working the streets was far lower in NYC compared to Bogota, but it wasn't as if these girls were trading up for the good life. They were still subjected to violence and abuse regardless of geographic location. And this 'protection' that Mandy spoke of? A pimp that would more than likely get her hooked on crack to control her and keep her docile. She may be young and pretty now, but after a few years of smoking crack and working the streets for days on end, she would become something else entirely. Eventually, her earning power would be next to nothing and the pimp would simply cast her out. Mandy would be resigned to performing whatever deplorable sexual acts were demanded of her just to get her next hit. She would continue doing this until the day her body rotted from the inside out.

"And what… what did they ask from you in return? If they were offering you safe passage to the United States, what did you have to do for them?" Drake asked.

Mandy flushed and averted her eyes. While Drake waited for the woman to reply, Screech returned and handed him a glass of Scotch. Surprised by the amount—the rock glass was nearly full—Drake raised an eyebrow and turned to face his partner.

Screech wasn't even looking at him; he was sipping an equally tall glass of Scotch.

For someone so adamant that they needed to vacate the premises, to lay low until DI Palmer's witch hunt was over, Screech hadn't been shy with the alcohol.

Drake returned his gaze to Mandy.

"Mandy, we're not here to—"

The girl's eyes shot up.

"For a week before we left, they made us eat these vegetables—huge plates of peas and corn. You know the small kind? Chopped up?"

Drake nodded and encouraged her to continue.

It sounded to him like the bags of frozen vegetables that you got from the supermarket freezer.

"They made us eat so much of it… I almost puked every night. But they told us that if we didn't eat it all, we wouldn't get on the boat. Then, on the last night, they came to us with these plastic bags and told us we had to swallow them all."

"Competitive eating," Screech muttered.

Drake turned.

"What?"

"The peas and carrots... they're for stretching the stomach. It's a common tactic among competitive eaters."

Drake made a face.

Gee, interesting factoid, Screech, but let's just try to keep focused, okay?

"Mandy, can you tell us what happened to the other girls? Why they died?"

Mandy took her time responding.

"At first... at first, I thought the powder in the bags was cocaine, but... Drake, they told us to drink this horrible stuff, but some of the girls couldn't do it. I think it was... I think it was to keep the baggies from breaking during the trip. I tried to make my friend Stacy drink it, but she kept vomiting... at one point, she vomited so hard that I thought she was going to puke up the baggies. And then, not long after we were moved from the boat to the shipping container, she started to foam at the mouth and shake. I knew then that the baggies weren't full of cocaine—I've been around the stuff my whole life and never seen anyone act like that." She took a deep, hitching breath. "And then it started to happen to all of them."

Drake swallowed hard as the final pieces of Mandy's story fell into place. Not only were these bastards shipping the whores from Colombia, but were using them as drug mules as well.

And it was painfully obvious which was more valuable to them.

Mandy was right about the powder, as well; it wasn't cocaine. In the past fifteen years, Colombia's heroin production had gone from negligible to becoming the US's main supplier of the poison.

"Mandy, can you tell me if the bag had any sort of marking on it? A symbol or design?"

The girl looked momentarily confused, but that slowly started to nod.

"A snake... a snake eating a ball, or the earth, maybe."

Screech sputtered and Drake once again turned to look at him.

The man's eyes were wide, his lips and chin wet with Scotch. Sometimes Drake forgot that this was all new for him, that he was just a computer analyst who had seen too much in too short a period of time.

"Screech, why don't you go take a walk and come back in ten. I can handle it from here."

Screech didn't look at Drake; his eyes were locked on Mandy's.

"I'm fine," he said dryly.

Drake very much doubted his partner's claim, but he was in no position to argue. He had to get as much information out of Mandy while he still could.

"What about the boat? Anything special you can remember about it? How about the container you were transferred into?" Drake asked.

Again, Mandy hesitated, but this time she shook her head.

"I was blindfolded for most of the time, and when we were told we could remove the blindfold, it was always dark."

"And when they opened the container... did you see what the men looked like? What about where you were... did you recognize anything?"

It was a stretch of course; the likelihood of a working girl from Colombia knowing what part of the New York she'd landed on was slim to none.

"I was so scared... I heard two men talking... one with a Russian or European accent and the other Spanish... and when they were deep in the container checking the other girls, I just got up and ran. The only thing I remember was a square building that looked like it was made out of metal."

Now it was Drake's brow that furrowed.

Russian and Spanish accents... a building made of metal...

"One more thing, Mandy—I just have one more question for you."

Mandy nodded.

"The baggies... the drugs that you swallowed. They aren't... still in you, are they?"

Mandy turned red again and she shook her head.

"Then where are they?"

No answer this time; the girl simply hooked her chin toward the bathroom. Drake indicated for Screech to take a look. When he was out of earshot, Mandy leaned in close and whispered, "Drake, will you help me?"

Drake frowned.

"I *am* helping you," he said quietly. He was trying to extract however much information he could to pass along to Yasiv and his team, while it was still fresh in her mind.

Mandy shook her head vehemently.

"No, I mean help find the *bandejos* who did this to me. To get back at them for what they did to my sisters."

Drake opened his mouth to reply, but Screech emerged from the bathroom, his face pale, his lips pressed into a frown. In his arms were the baggies of heroin that Mandy had smuggled inside her body. There were so many of them, that they almost spilled over his thin arms with every step. Drake would never know how Mandy, as petite as she was, managed to get all of them inside her body.

No wonder the other girls died… just standing would cause the baggies to rub together. And the second there was just a small scratch, once the integrity of the plastic was broken, their stomach acid would slowly eat away at the rest.

"Drake? Will you help me find and kill the men that did this to us?"

Chapter 14

"**MANDY, I'M NOT SURE** where you got this idea... but I won't... I'm not going to *kill* anybody. Screech and I, we're private investigators, that's it."

"But they're scared of you, I heard—"

Drake shook his head.

"They should be scared, because we will find them—we'll find the people responsible. But we won't *kill* them, Mandy."

Beckett would, Screech thought suddenly. *Beckett would find out who did these horrible things and make them pay, just like he did Craig Sloan and Ray Reynolds and Donnie DiMarco.*

A pang of guilt hit Screech that was so strong that he had to grab the back of Drake's chair for support.

I'm responsible for this... I saw the drugs on the yacht, on B-Yacht'ch. I saw the girls.

His mind flicked back to his short time in the Virgin Gorda.

I even know the drink she's speaking of... the girls were drinking it on the yacht. What did Beckett say? It was to neutralize the stomach acid to stop the baggies from being dissolved.

Shit, he and Beckett had even been complicit: they'd taken the boat from a bad man in Donnie DiMarco and gifted it to someone even worse in Bob Bumacher.

Screech swallowed hard.

"Drake, can I talk to you in the family room for a second?"

Drake nodded.

"Mandy, you'll be okay here. Just stay put and we'll be right back."

Mandy didn't reply, but she didn't protest either and the two men left the bedroom. When they were on the other side of the kitchen, Screech spoke in a hushed tone.

"Drake, there's something that you should know... about the photo—"

Drake stopped him by holding up a hand.

"Is this about the shit that happened at Triple D before the Reynolds farm? Because I saw the pictures. I know about Donnie and I know about the boat. Screech... we all have our reasons for—"

"No, you don't understand. I think that the yacht, B-yacht'ch, is the one that she was transported on—the same one that we found for Bob Bumacher."

Drake's eyes narrowed.

"Really? Why would you think that?"

Screech swallowed.

"Because we saw some things on there, some things that—"

"Okay, fuck, we don't have time for this shit. I'll look into it, okay?"

No, it's not okay, Screech thought. *None of this is okay.*

"Screech, I'll look into it. But you said yourself we need to get moving," Drake cleared his throat before continuing. "Now, this shit about two men with Russian and Spanish accents... the ones who mentioned me and the Skeleton King. Do you think they could be related to the Church of Liberation? To ANGUIS Holdings?"

The question surprised Screech and it took him a few moments to catch his bearings.

"I think... *maybe*. I sorta recall a couple of Russian sounding names on the list of officers for ANGUIS Holdings."

Among a couple hundred more, he thought, but didn't say.

"If these guys are shipping girls and heroin from overseas, this isn't just some small-scale operation. I'm guessing that ninety percent of the names on the list that you dug up are just bit players—people that received payouts or whatnot.

Like Detective Simmons and…" Drake's sentence trailed off, but Screech knew exactly what the man was thinking.

Like Detective Simmons and Clay Cuthbert…

"And these payouts were all funneled and disguised through the Church of Liberation," Drake continued. "Now that the church is dead, let's hope that they slip up and transfer money that we can more easily follow. If they do, this will tell us who's really in charge of ANGUIS. You think you can work on this?"

Screech was taken aback. Despite what Drake had been through over the past week or so, it appeared that the man hadn't missed a beat. Clearly, the downtime hadn't been spent twiddling his thumbs; he'd been thinking.

Drake snapped his fingers.

"Hey, Screech? You alive in there?"

"Y-y-yeah. I'll look into it."

"Good. Now that other thing Mandy mentioned… the metal building?"

"What about it?"

"What the hell is a 'metal building' to you? A skyscraper?"

"I'd say a skyscraper is more glass than anything else."

Drake frowned.

"Yeah, but you're not a scared girl from Colombia. I'd say—wait. *Wait.*"

"What? What is it?"

"I went to a metal building once with Raul and it was by the water."

"*With* Raul?"

Drake waved a hand.

"Never mind that—it was a hangar of sorts, for fixing up planes or something. And it was made of corrugated metal."

There was an excited look in his eyes now. "Do you still have the list of buildings that ANGUIS Holdings owns in the city?"

"Raul? You were with—"

"Fuck, Screech, do you have the document or not?"

Screech felt his frustration rising. He supposed that he should be used to this by now—to living outside of Drake's world, the one that only took place inside his head. But he wasn't. And now that he had his own demons haunting him, Screech felt poorly equipped to deal with any of this.

But Drake was right; they didn't have much time.

Screech strode over to the desk in the corner of the room and pulled the top drawer open. After rooting through some files, he held up several sheets of paper that were stapled together.

Drake grabbed it from him and quickly started flipping through the pages.

"Any of these—"

Both men suddenly froze when the sound of sirens wafted in through the open window. They held their breath as they waited for it to pass; this was Manhattan, after all. But when it grew steadily louder, Screech felt his heart start to race. Without saying a word, he slunk over to the window and parted the blinds with two fingers.

Then he let them snap closed and whipped around to face Drake.

"They're right outside!" he hissed. "Drake, there are officers right outside!"

Drake swore and rolled up the piece of paper and jammed it into his pocket.

"Is there another way out of here? A way to get out without using the front door?"

Screech nodded.

"Through the bedroom; the window leads to a small balcony and from there you can—"

Drake suddenly sprinted for the bedroom. But when he pushed the door open, both of them paused.

The window was already open and Mandy was no longer sitting on the bed.

"Mandy?" Screech said. "Mandy?"

He glanced around the room, but she was nowhere to be seen. He checked the closet, then looked under the bed.

"Drake, she's not—"

But Screech was alone. He sighed heavily and picked up his glass of Scotch from the table.

"You're welcome," he muttered bitterly as he drank the last sip. "Both of you."

Chapter 15

DRAKE HOPPED FROM SCREECH'S balcony to the neighbors and landed with a wince. His side flared with pain, and he was reminded of what Dr. Ramsey had said about taking it easy and to stop drinking.

Well, he thought glumly, *oh for two.*

From the neighbor's balcony, he managed to hoist himself around the other side, then pull himself onto the roof. Crouching, he paused for a moment to catch his breath and to look for Mandy.

He didn't see her anywhere.

It had crossed his mind on more than one occasion that this whole Mandy thing was a ruse, an elaborate setup orchestrated by DI Palmer to rein him in. If this were the case, the bags of heroin were a nice touch, a good way to get solid evidence on him and Screech.

But kill?

Mandy had been clear on that point: she wanted Drake to kill the people responsible for what had happened to her.

Drake didn't think that Palmer would bat an eye at planting evidence or taking a payout, but effectively contracting a hit—albeit on an unknown assailant at this time—that was too far… wasn't it?

Drake stayed low as he made his way across the roof and then peered over the side.

Two police officers had just emerged from their squad car and were making their way toward the front entrance of Screech's building.

He waited for them to enter the apartment lobby and then hurried down the fire escape. The stairs were rickety and unstable, but he moved quickly enough so as to avoid anybody spotting him if they glanced out their windows. Grateful that he parked his conspicuous Crown Vic in an alley behind the building, Drake kept his head low as he hurried over to it and got inside.

Then the pain really started. It was as if someone were poking the right side of his body with hundreds of glowing hot needles. To top it off, he was sweating profusely and was having a hard time catching his breath.

Despite the urgent need to get as far away from Screech's apartment as possible, Drake was forced to close his eyes and wait for the symptoms to pass. It took nearly a full minute before he could open them again. And when he did, he wasted no time in pulling the sheets of paper that Screech had given him from his pocket.

"Come on," he grumbled as he quickly scanned the list of addresses. And then, halfway down the third page, he jabbed a finger at a specific line.

"Bingo," he whispered.

Just as he put the car into drive, a voice from the backseat spoke up.

"What did you find?"

Drake whipped around, leading with his hand. At the last second, he managed to modify the arc of his blow so that he didn't strike Mandy in the face and instead hit the back of the seat.

"What the fuck—what the fuck are you doing here?" he gasped.

Mandy leaned back, a confused expression on her face.

"I heard the cops, and I don't—I think they might be involved, too."

Drake ground his teeth and turned his gaze out the window. He half expected to see the officers coming at him, their weapons drawn.

But there was no one out there.

"What did you find?" Mandy repeated. "Do you know who did this?"

An image of the airplane hangar that he'd been drawn to by Raul, where the impish man had tied Ivan Meitzer up to a chair and beaten him came to mind. *That* had been a metal building and it was near the water. In fact, Drake even thought he remembered seeing several shipping containers on the same property.

And that address was also on the list of buildings owned by ANGUIS Holdings.

"*Know*? No, I don't *know*," he grumbled. "But I have a pretty damn good idea."

Chapter 16

"WOW, YOU GUYS ALMOST look like real cops. But, alas, you've got the wrong address. The bachelorette party's down the hall."

The two police officers, who had introduced themselves as Officer Derek and Officer Galmond, exchanged looks before turning back to Screech.

"Have you been drinking tonight?" Officer Derek asked.

Screech held the glass of scotch close to the man's face, sniffing as he did. Officer Derek gently pushed it away.

"Is that a crime now, too? Is it illegal to have a drink on one's birthday?" Screech asked, his speech slurred.

"Stephen, we're just here to ask you if you've seen your friend Damien Drake."

Screech took a sip of his drink, or tried to; it was empty. He shrugged.

"Haven't seen him in months. Last I heard, he was on Dancing with the Stars."

Officer Galmond, who was significantly larger than his partner, stepped forward and fully blocked the doorway.

"How 'bout you stop fucking around and tell us where Drake is, huh? Save us all a headache."

Screech held his ground.

"You know what? You might be right. It wasn't Dancing with the Stars." He smacked his forehead with the palm of his free hand. "I'm an idiot. It was Survivor. Yeah, that's right, Survivor; the 384th season of Survivor, where the contestants are left naked on an island. They are forced to fight each other, while at the same time, they're trying to migrate through a giant maze. And—get this—the judge? A giant purple guy who wants to put rings on his gloves to rule the universe. How about that?"

Officer Galmond stepped forward again, and this time Screech retreated into his apartment.

"Hey, wait a second—aren't you guys like vampires?"

Officer Derek raised an eyebrow.

"Vampires? What have you been smoking?"

Screech nodded to himself.

"Yeah, you guys *are* like vampires... you can't come in here unless I *invite* you in. I'm right, aren't I? Tell me I'm right, Scott Rogowsky. Please, Quizmaster, tell me that I won HQ for once in my measly existence."

Officer Galmond snarled.

"How about I cite probable cause because you've got a joint on the table over there, huh? I mean, you certainly are acting like you're high."

Screech ignored the comment.

"I *would* invite you in, but you know what? I just ran out of douche bag tea and asshole pie. So maybe you can come back tomorrow."

With that, Screech reached for the door and started to close it. Except Officer Galmond's foot got in the way.

"Oh, one more thing," Screech said, no longer slurring his words. "You see that over there? Yeah, right there, on the kitchen counter? That's a camera. So, before you go and do something stupid, Officers Gandalf and Griswold, know that you're being recorded."

Officer Derek reached over and gave his partner a nudge.

"If we find out that you've seen Drake, we'll arrest you for conspiracy."

Screech nodded and then waved as the two men started to walk backward down the hallway.

"*Buh-bye.* And, please, don't let the door hit you on the ass on the way out."

When the officers made it to the elevator, Screech finally closed the door. Then he collapsed against it, breathing heavily.

Even though he'd played it cool, and was quite proud of the charade, the entire time he'd been terrified. With a hard swallow, he walked over to the counter and picked up the TV remote control.

"Fucking douche bag thought that this was a camera?" he muttered. Heart still racing, he reached down and opened the cupboard beneath the sink.

There, stuffed haphazardly in a grocery bag, were the balls of heroin that Mandy had left in his bathroom. His first inclination had been to flush them, but at the last moment, he'd decided against it. It dawned on him that he and Drake might need them later.

After another deep breath, Screech pulled out his cell phone. He briefly considered calling Drake, but he didn't know how far his partner was from the officers that were likely searching around the building at this very moment. The last thing he wanted to do, was to set off the man's phone when he was sneaking by them.

Instead, he pulled up Beckett's contact information. They hadn't spoken since their interaction at the Reynolds's farm, and before that, it had been in the Virgin Gorda.

When I took the photos of him… of him staring down at Donnie DiMarco as the man drowned.

Screech shuddered.

He didn't want to call Beckett; he didn't like the look in the man's eyes. And yet, they were responsible for this mess.

Somewhere out there was a shipping crate, and inside were the bodies of nearly two dozen girls.

And for that, someone had to pay. Drake would do his best to find those responsible, to bring them to justice, but he would only go so far. Beckett, on the other hand, had no such limits.

With a swallow, Screech hit send and a moment later a male voice answered.

"Beckett? It's Screech. I think… I think we need to meet up."

Chapter 17

DRAKE FLICKED OFF THE headlights before turning down the narrow road that led to the abandoned airport hangar. He was on high alert now, his eyes whipping back and forth, searching for any signs that this might be a setup. If it wasn't, if Mandy's story was true, it would be equally as dangerous.

On first blush, the place looked deserted, but it had appeared that way the first time Drake had been here. Only then Raul and Ivan had been inside.

A hint of movement in the rearview caught his eye, and he slowed even further. It was only Mandy shifting in her seat, but this reminded him that he wasn't alone. The last thing that he'd wanted was to bring her with him, but he saw no other way around it. The girl was right: she couldn't go to the police, not with the apparent links to ANGUIS Holdings. There was only one, maybe two people in the NYPD that Drake thought he could trust, but bringing them in now would only serve to put them in DI Palmer's crosshairs. No, he would reserve his connections for when he had no other choice.

Taking Mandy back to Screech's was also out of the question; the police were almost certainly staking the place out and they were most likely doing the same at Jasmine's. Even if they weren't, he'd had a hard enough time explaining what had happened at the farm… bringing a young, attractive girl with an even more outlandish story than his own would be a next to impossible sell.

Drake eased his Crown Vic to a stop beside the hangar and then reached into the glovebox and pulled out his pistol. He jammed it into the back of his pants and then turned to face Mandy.

"You stay here," he instructed. He debated giving her the keys, but decided against it. Mandy had already run from Screech's without a word and Drake didn't to want risk getting stranded here by himself, especially if it was a setup. Besides, the woman had made it all the way to Triple D on foot without ever having been to New York before. She could handle herself just fine, he surmised, if it came to that.

Which he most definitely hoped it did not.

"If I'm not back in about fifteen minutes, you get out of the car and keep walking. See the city lights over there? The ones tightly packed in a circle? That's the hospital. Just follow the signs with the big capital 'H's on them. You go to the hospital and ask for Dr. Beckett Campbell. Tell him that I sent you. Do you understand?"

Mandy nodded and Drake turned his gaze back to the windshield.

"Does any of this look familiar to you? Is this the metal building you remember?"

Mandy chewed her lip.

"I don't think so… it was dark and the building was more… I dunno, *black*. This is more silver."

Drake focused on the corrugated metal door at the front of the hangar. It was indeed silver as Mandy said, but he wasn't ready to write this place off just yet. The woman herself admitted that she'd been frightened and that her memory of what had happened after she'd risen from the dead wasn't good. And this place made *sense*. For one, it was owned by ANGUIS and he'd already been here once with Raul of all people. Second, it was on the water, and third, while it had been devoid of planes when he'd been here last, it at least had the capacity to store them.

And if you're shipping cargo—human or otherwise—access to planes would be a definite asset.

No... this is *the place. It* has *to be.*

Drake nodded and opened the door.

"All right, stay here—I'm going inside. Remember: if I'm not back in fifteen, go to the hospital and ask for Dr. Beckett Campbell."

With that, Drake stepped out into the night.

Chapter 18

"**AND YOU THINK THIS** is all somehow related to Bob Bumacher and his boat? Sorry, his *yacht*?"

Screech looked down at his shoes as they walked. Even though Beckett had agreed to meet, he was none too pleased to actually go through with it. In fact, when Screech had first arrived at the man's office, he'd tried to open with some small talk, but Beckett had quickly shut him down. Screech had gone on to ask about his hand, to see how it was healing, but Beckett had just shrugged him off.

This was a very different Beckett than the one who had made hooker and blow jokes in the Virgin Gorda.

"It's the same insignia on the baggies as in the yacht," Screech offered.

Beckett shrugged.

"So, what? It's not unusual for these things to be cut up and repackaged with different brands on them. This isn't like Denzel Washington in American Gangster—there's not just one provider, one source anymore. There is no guarantee that the stuff that you have is even from the same country as the stuff that Donnie had on the yacht."

Screech nodded as Beckett spoke. What the man was saying was reasonable and probable, and yet he couldn't help but think that it just wasn't accurate. Everything that had happened since he was hired to work at Triple D—maybe even before that, when the DA had come to strike a deal to get his brother out of prison—was all connected.

Drake was right; it all boiled down to Ken Smith and ANGUIS Holdings.

"But let's say it *is* connected," Beckett said. "Why'd you come to me with this?"

Screech was surprised by the question and stopped walking. The street was nearly empty, as the last classes on campus ended several hours ago, it was unusually quiet and serene for New York City. And this suddenly made Screech uncomfortable.

Was it smart coming to Beckett? Given what I've seen him do?

"I had no one else to go to," he said at last. It wasn't a complete lie, but it was far from the whole truth.

Beckett looked him up and down and then ran a hand through his hair.

"You sure that's why?"

Screech's thoughts flicked back to what Mandy had said in his apartment, that she wanted Drake to kill the people responsible for the shipping container disaster.

"Yeah," he said with a swallow. "I had no one else to go to. The police are after Drake and he's in hiding."

Beckett started walking again and Screech stayed by the man's side. For a minute or more, neither of them spoke.

Screech tried not to let his mind wander, but he kept thinking about the look in Beckett's eyes. The cold, empty stare that he'd seen after Beckett had bashed Craig Sloan's head in with a stone and as Donnie DiMarco struggled for air.

"I'll tell you what, you bring a bag with you?" Beckett asked unexpectedly.

Screech nodded and reached into his pocket to squeeze the baggy within.

"All right, hand it over. I'll bring it to the lab and see if I can trace the source, for what it's worth."

Screech looked around to confirm that they were alone before pulling out the baggy. He cupped it in his hand and then awkwardly extended his wrist like a handicapped person attempting their first ever handshake.

"Okay, Scarface, it's a couple of grams of heroin, not a fucking kilo of cocaine. Just give it to me," Beckett raised his right hand and wiggled his nub of a middle finger. "Besides, I think my days of the ol' secret handshake and finger wags are over, don't you?"

Screech nodded and quickly handed the bag over. Beckett slipped it into his pocket.

"You're not... you're not going to *use* it, are you?"

Beckett frowned.

"I may have had a bump or two on Donnie's yacht, but I'm not a goddamn heroin addict, Screech. Keep it together, man."

Screech nodded. He didn't think that Beckett was an addict, of course, but he'd seen stranger things in his time. He'd seen his own brother Larry function normally even after consuming enough Quaaludes to put a grizzly bear in a coma.

"And you say these girls... you say they all... they all *died*?" Beckett continued.

Screech nodded.

"Mandy said that they were forced to eat the bags of heroin. They were also told to drink this special cocktail... she said that it was terrible... terrible and bitter. Do you think—"

Beckett grabbed his arm and squeezed.

"Let it go, Screech," the man warned. Screech tried to pull away, but Beckett's grip held fast. "Just let it go. Nothing happened in the Virgin Gorda. *Nothing*."

And then, for a split second, Beckett's eyes went empty like they had done with Craig Sloan and Donnie DiMarco.

"Sorry," Screech grumbled, and Beckett released him.

They started walking again.

"All right," Beckett said, his tone returning to normal. "I'll take the *H* and run it through mass spec, determine its country of origin. I'll also keep my eye out for any girls that OD'd and come into the morgue. That's the most I can do for now. IA is still on my ass… making sure that I dot my t's and cross my i's, if you know what I mean."

Screech nodded. In truth, this was more than he expected from the man. Without any bodies, all they had to go on was a terrified girl's story.

And a pound of heroin. There was always that.

"Thanks, Beckett. Like I said, I had no one else to go to."

Beckett nodded and then turned to head back to his office. He only took three or four steps, however, before stopping again.

"Hey, Screech?"

"Yeah?"

"You didn't happen to take any pictures while you were on vacation, did you?"

Screech's heart skipped a beat.

"No," he lied. "Why do you ask?"

Beckett made a face.

"No reason. No reason at all. You take care yourself now, okay? And look out for that asshole Drake."

Chapter 19

THE HANGAR WAS EMPTY—*really* empty this time. There was no one tied up, no Raul lurking in the shadows. There was... nothing. The chair that Ivan had been bound to was gone and the light that Raul had used to disorient Drake when he'd initially entered the place was also absent.

In fact, the place looked immaculate, much cleaner than the first time he'd been there.

And yet, Drake was unconvinced. He stayed close to the wall as he made his way around the interior. It was dark inside, but not pitch; splinters of moonlight eked in through the many windows high above.

Keeping his ears perked and his eyes peeled, Drake continued to shuffle along, primed to react if Raul or anyone else—a man with a Russian accent, perhaps—leaped from the shadows. Eventually, he made it to the other side without being accosted. There was a corrugated metal door on this side, directly across from the one he'd entered through.

But while the front had been unlocked, this one appeared secured with a chain and padlock. It wasn't a tight seal, however; the metal near the bottom was bent just enough for a man about Drake's size to squeeze through. After peeking out to make sure that there was nobody standing there, Drake crouched and forced his way outside.

He nearly gasped at the pain that ripped up his midsection, but by some miracle managed to keep his lips pressed firmly together.

Dr. Ramsey wasn't lying... I am in rough shape.

After the pain subsided, Drake rose to his full height.

The first thing he noticed was the smell of salt in the air. The second was the sound of waves splashing on the shore not a hundred feet from where he stood. The third was the blue storage container lying between the back of the hangar and the shore.

Adrenaline flooded his system and Drake readied himself for action. But just like in the hangar, the gravel expanse to the shore appeared deserted. He crouched low and hurried across the gravel before pulling up behind an outcropping of rocks.

There he waited, once again listening for the sound of anyone following him. But the only things he heard were his own labored breathing and blood coursing through his ears. And maybe his liver crying out. The good news was that he could ignore all of these things—especially the latter, which he'd done for years.

Drake waited for a thirty count before continuing toward the shipping container. This time when he moved, he pulled the gun from the back of his pants and held it out in front of him. Another thirty count and he found himself leaning against the ass end of the container. This time when he paused, he realized that there were other sounds filling the night. He could hear the ocean, but beneath that, he could also make out something else; a hum of some sort, or a mechanical purr.

And it was getting louder.

Brow furrowed, Drake strafed his way along the metal container. He was halfway to the front when the shadows broke and he saw that the container was hanging open.

A second later, he noticed something in the water.

What in the fuck?

With a deep breath, Drake finally stepped out in the moonlight.

And then he stopped cold.

The mechanical purr that he'd been hearing was the sound of an outboard motor, which was attached to a large open top boat. Inside, Drake saw a stack of thick black bags that could only be filled with one thing.

Bodies.

A man with broad shoulders and gray hair suddenly stepped out into the open, a cigarette dangling from between his lips. He was mumbling something in a language that Drake didn't recognize and as he watched, the man reached down and wrapped a meaty hand on the corner of one of the bags. With a grunt, he started dragging the body bag across the small stretch of gravel between the opening of the shipping container and the boat.

Another grunt and the man hoisted the bag onto one shoulder and then tossed it on top of the others. It landed with a sickening thud that sent the boat rocking.

The man started to turn and Drake leveled the pistol at his chest.

"I'm thinking you should put your hands in the air," he said calmly.

The man, half turned now, froze, but his hands remained at his sides.

"I said, put your goddamn hands in the air," Drake repeated.

The man took a drag of the cigarette between his lips, but still refused to raise his hands. He also looked to be smirking.

"I said, put your—"

The man was thick and stocky, but also quick. As he exhaled a thick cloud of smoke, his right hand snaked behind him.

He was quick, but Drake was quicker.

He fired a single shot. Drake had been aiming for the man's knee, but before he squeezed the trigger, his liver revolted and the muscles on the right side of his body clenched.

The bullet struck the man just below the hip.

He grunted, but didn't go down. He did, however, stop reaching for whatever was in the back of his pants and raised his hands. Drake was amazed that the man had taken the bullet with just a grunt, but he didn't let this distract him.

"I want you to—"

"Drake!" Someone shouted behind him. "Drop the fucking gun!"

Drake's shoulders sagged. He'd put himself in the worst position possible. The second he took his eyes off the man in front of him—who was, unbelievably, still smirking and smoking—he would either pull his gun or make a run for the boat. But if Drake didn't do as he was asked, a bullet would find its way between his shoulder blades.

A smarter man, one more prepared, one who wasn't still fighting the effects of methanol poisoning, perhaps, would have moved to the front of the open container so that no one could sneak up from behind.

"Turn around now, Drake, or I swear to god, I'll put a bullet in your spine."

He had no choice; besides, it was better to face death when it came, and not get bumrushed by it.

Grinding his teeth, Drake dropped his gun and spun around.

"You? What the fuck are *you* doing here?"

PART II

A Business Card, a Scalpel, and an Auction

Chapter 20

THE CIGAR SMOKE WAS so thick in the room that it was difficult to see the three people sitting beside him, let alone the two across.

There was a nervous tension in the air as well, something that Ken Smith was not accustomed to. So far, everything had fallen in place exactly the way he'd planned it. Well, not exactly; there had been issues with Ray Reynolds and the Church of Liberation, things that he was still in the process of cleaning up. But once DI Palmer brought Drake in, the loose ends would all be nicely tied up.

That is, until the issues with the package.

"I thought that this was under control," Ken hissed. "And you are sure that all twenty-one of the girls are dead, Bob?"

The bald man across from him raised his head. He had at least five inches and fifty pounds of solid muscle on Ken, but it was the former who looked terrified.

"Y-yes, Mayor Smith. All— "

The man to Ken's left, a man with a dark beard and bespoke suit, leaned in close to the mayor's ear and whispered something.

Ken nodded and turned back to Bob.

"There were twenty-two girls who boarded the yacht in *Riohacha*, Bob, not twenty-one. Maybe we need to get someone more competent to take care of the logistics."

Bob's eyes went wide.

"No, sir. E-e-everything went according to plan. The girls were loaded onto the yacht, and then—"

Ken slammed his fist down on the table, and the two men across from him jumped.

"Everything went according to *plan*? *Seriously?* Bob, you imbecile, we've got an auction coming up and not only do I not have any product, but I've got the police snooping around. What part of the *plan* was that?"

"I thought the police—"

Ken slammed his fist down on the table again, this time so hard that his cigar fell out of the ashtray.

"Don't think! I don't pay you to think!" he bellowed. Behind Bob, Ken saw a flicker of movement; Raul had stepped from the shadows, just in case. He waved him off and turned to the man beside Bob. "What about my drugs? Could they be salvaged from the girls?"

This man raised his head, but unlike Bob who was gripped by fear, he only looked loathsome.

"I have no idea. I got you both the girls and the dope. That was my part of the bargain—I told you that the baggies weren't designed for such a long journey. I *warned* you. But you didn't listen. Now, I've fulfilled my end of the bargain. The rest… the dead girls… that's on you and Bob, not me."

Bob growled, but Raul made his presence known and cooler heads prevailed.

Warned me? Nobody warns me.

Ken picked his cigar off the table and took several puffs.

"I need you to get me a dozen more girls and more heroin. That's what I paid you for, and you failed to deliver. Don't you forget what I can do to your brother, Dane."

Dane scowled.

"I upheld my part of the bargain. As for Damien, he's all over the news. You've already ruined whatever reputation he's got left," the man fired back.

Ken cursed under his breath. DI Palmer was supposed to wait until he got confirmation that the shipment had arrived safe and sound before going after Drake. But that asshole had become Chatty Kathy in front of the camera.

Both Drake brothers had proved valuable, but Ken was beginning to think that they were more trouble than they were worth.

He would be happy when they were finally gone.

"It's not just Drake you need to worry about," Ken said, taking another puff of his cigar.

Dane Drake smiled.

"Me? You think that I have anything left to lose? If so, you're sorely—"

Ken shook his head.

"It appears as if your brother's girlfriend is expecting," he said calmly.

Something in Dane's face broke, and now it was Ken's turn to smile.

"I'll get you another shipment," Dane hissed. "But this is the last one."

More insolence.

You will do what I ask until I *am done with you.*

"This time you are taking someone with you."

Dane Drake shook his head.

"That's not part of the deal. They're my contacts in Colombia and I'll keep it that way."

"Two dozen dead Colombian girls and fifty keys of missing heroin wasn't part of the deal, either. Bob will take whoever I say with you to Colombia. And this time when you return, I want my girls alive and my drugs in bags, not in their bloodstream. There will be no third time."

Again, Dane looked as if he were going to protest, but bit his tongue.

"Now get the fuck out of my sight," Ken barked.

The two men rose and exited the room. When they were gone, Ken brought the cigar to his lips and took a puff. It suddenly tasted bitter to him, and he butted it out.

When the man to his left spoke again, this time he didn't bother disguising his words.

"I've got my men cleaning up the mess at the hangar."

Ken nodded.

"What about the auction? Do we have enough product?"

The man hesitated before answering.

"I can scrape something together for the time being. It won't be the same, but..."

"...it's the best we can do for now," Ken finished for him. Then he turned to the sharply dressed woman to his left and the tanned man with the shaved head on her other side. "Anything you'd like to add?"

They both shook their heads, but Ken could see the displeasure on their faces.

"Good," he said, before looking at Raul. "Go get Wesley. Tell him to go with Dane, find out who his connections are in

Colombia. And then, after the girls and drugs have been loaded into the container, have him shoot Dane in the head."

Raul nodded and Ken pulled a new cigar from his suit jacket pocket.

After Dane was gone, that would only leave one Drake left. But Damien, Ken knew, would most likely prove more difficult to snuff out.

Chapter 21

"HE'S LOADING BODIES IN the boat! You need to—"

The man in the NYPD uniform aimed the pistol a little higher.

"Drake, I swear to God, if you say another word, I'm gonna blow your head off."

Drake bit his lip. He wanted nothing more than to tell this little prick off, but he didn't like the way the man's hand was trembling.

"Good. Now, I want you to walk slowly towards me. Keep your hands in the air."

Drake had no choice but to obey. Even though he had bested the man in their previous altercation, he was still game. There was no question in Drake's mind that if he decided to do anything but as instructed, his penance would be lead.

"Good," the man said. "Now I want you to—"

A shadow suddenly appeared behind the officer and Drake cringed. Sensing that something was up, the officer's brow furrowed and he started to turn.

"No! Wait!" Drake shouted, but it was too late.

The much smaller figure swung something heavy in a wide arc. It struck the officer across the cheek and smashed into his nose. He grunted, then collapsed to the gravel in a heap.

Drake immediately whipped around, his eyes desperately seeking the man who was filling the boat with bodies.

"Shit!"

The short bastard with the gray hair that Drake had winged must have bolted the second his back was to him. He was already halfway across the bay and even weighed down with the bodies, the boat was putting more distance between them with every second that passed.

Drake swore again then turned to see what had happened to Officer Paul Kramer.

"Is he alive?" he asked as he strode toward the downed officer. Mandy, who looked as terrified as she'd been when Drake had first met her at Screech's apartment, dropped the tire iron as he approached.

Paul Kramer was an asshole, but Drake still felt some responsibility for him, considering that he had been a part of Clay's life. A quick inspection answered his initial query: he had a broken nose and maybe even a fractured cheek, but Paul Kramer was very much alive.

Drake raised his eyes and stared at Mandy.

"I told you to stay in the fucking car."

"I'm sorry," Mandy said softly, and Drake instantly regretted yelling at her. She was just scared... and she might have just saved his life.

"It's okay," he replied, looking around. There were no police sirens or lights filling the night. However Kramer had found him, he'd done so alone.

That was good.

Confident that they were alone for the time being, Drake turned his attention to the shipping container that the Russian was in the process of cleaning when he'd arrived.

Even illuminated by only the weak light from his flashlight, what Drake saw almost made him sick. It wasn't the blood that coated the floor of the container, nor the congealed pools of vomit in the corners. No, it was the knowledge that less than 24 hours ago there were nearly two dozen living and breathing Colombian girls locked in the dark. All they wanted was a better life for themselves, and what did they get for their efforts? Unintentional overdose, followed by a watery grave.

Drake looked away—he couldn't stare at the mess any longer.

Without saying a word to Mandy—who looked legitimately terrified now—Drake grabbed Officer Kramer by the ankles and started to drag him across the gravel. Kramer was on the smaller size, but Drake's body protested even the smallest of physical movement now. With a pained grunt, he somehow managed to hoist the officer into the shipping container. Kramer's head bounced off the metal and his eyes rolled forward.

"Wha-wha-what? What happened?" he muttered.

Drake didn't answer; instead, he slammed the doors closed and then used the tire iron that Mandy had struck Kramer with to lock them.

"Did I do something wrong?" Mandy asked quietly. "I thought he was going to kill you, Drake."

Drake sighed.

"No, you didn't do anything wrong," he replied. *But you most definitely put us in a jam*, he thought, but didn't say.

Any bullshit that DI Palmer might have on him for what happened at the Reynolds farm, or any of the shit he'd done during Smith's campaign, Drake thought he might be able to weasel his way out of.

But this… this was going to prove difficult, maybe even impossible, to get away from unscathed.

He needed to call someone, someone who had some sway in the police department. Someone he could fully trust.

Only he didn't know anyone like that. All the people he knew were *ifs, ands, buts.* Maybes. Sometimes.

But given the situation, Drake had no choice.

He took his cellphone out of his pocket and with a heavy sigh, started to dial.

Chapter 22

SCREECH STARED BLANKLY AT his computer screen until his eyes started to defocus. He knew that he should be trying to trace the money that was moving in and out of ANGUIS Holdings as Drake had suggested, but he couldn't bring himself to do it.

Not yet, anyway.

Instead, he found himself staring at familiar photographs.

There was the photo of Beckett standing over Donnie DiMarco as he drowned, the picture of the bricks of heroin in the yacht. And then there was the photograph of Beckett holding the stone covered in blood moments after he'd brained Craig Sloan.

He'd taken all of these.

The second set of photographs were taken by someone else: Drake in an election office, Drake holding a finger bone, Drake in the 62nd precinct evidence room. There was even a photograph taken outside of Peter Kellington's house moments before Clay had been killed. And then there was the photo of Drake on his knees, weeping, his mouth wide, Clay's bloody body in his arms.

But perhaps the most disturbing image wasn't of Drake at all. It was of a younger, smiling Jasmine holding what Screech now knew to be a key of heroin.

A photo that he was never supposed to see. In fact, all of these new images were meant for select eyes only. But Screech had his means.

It wasn't easy, even with the backdoor rootkit he'd installed on his cell phone before Ken and Raul had seized it. In fact, he'd been at a dead end until someone had plugged his phone directly into the USB drive instead of just transferring the images over Wi-Fi.

Screech rubbed his eyes. He was exhausted, but knew that he wouldn't be able to sleep. Sleep had become an adversary ever since he'd started at Triple D, and now, after what had transpired in the Virgin Gorda, it had become his archnemesis.

He sighed and then minimized the folders with the images. He would figure out what to do with them later. Right now, he had to help Drake. And, while the man was a dinosaur, it quickly became apparent that he was onto something: with the Church of Liberation's financials frozen, there might very well be a traceable money trail out there somewhere.

And, with remote access to Ken Smith's computer, it didn't take Screech long to find it.

He had to give the man credit; Ken had been careful. ANGUIS had made dozens of transfers since the events at the Reynolds farm, but all had been of moderate sums, sums that wouldn't raise eyebrows. But as Screech dug deeper, he discovered that after being routed through several international banks, they eventually found their way into just four accounts.

And once he had the account numbers, he was able to cross-reference them with all the names that were listed on the ANGUIS Holdings accounting statements. A little brute force hacking and Screech identified the names of the primary account holders.

"Steffani Loomis, Horatio Dupont, Boris Brackovich, and Mendes Corp.," Screech read out loud.

He tapped his chin and thought about these for a moment.

"Well, it looks like I found your Russian, Drake," he said, staring at Boris's name. But it was the last one that held his interest. Of the four, it was the only one that wasn't a personal account.

And there was only one Mendes that he was familiar with: Raul Mendes.

Eyebrows knitted, Screech went about trying to find more information about Mendes Corp. This proved considerably more difficult. For one, the account was held in the District of Colombia and even though this wasn't the 1980's heyday for drug lords, Screech still couldn't get his hands on anything more than the name.

All breadcrumbs led to… nowhere.

Frustrated, Screech pulled up the file folder on the desktop with Drake's name on it. Only this time he wasn't looking for a photo, but a video; the video from the camera that Drake had set up in the basement that had held the final Church of Liberation meeting.

He skipped forward to the part where DI Palmer met and spoke with Raul for several moments before parting ways.

Raul… Raul…

Screech drummed his fingers on his forehead. He was fairly certain that Ken Smith was at the head of all of this, despite none of the accounts leading back to him, but the person that kept popping up was Raul.

But why? What makes Raul so special?

Screech went back to his browser and started typing so quickly that his fingers became a blur. By searching for both Ken Smith and Raul Mendes, he came upon an article from a Colombian newspaper dated more than forty years ago.

And while Screech didn't speak let alone read Spanish, when he saw the accompanying photo, his jaw went slack.

"You've got to be shitting me," he said, reaching for his phone.

Chapter 23

DRAKE LEANED AGAINST THE side of the shipping container, gun at his hip, as the man with the cigarette in his mouth approached. The man moved slowly, but Drake didn't blame him; Officer Kramer had since awoken and was banging against the side of the container. It sounded like there was a mountain lion inside. He was shouting, too, but the words were muffled and Drake couldn't make them out.

Which, he thought, *is probably for the best.*

"Drake? Is that you?"

Drake stepped away from the container and showed the man the pistol in his hand.

"That's not necessary. I came alone, just as you asked," the man said, taking another drag. From behind him, Mandy stepped out, a piece of rebar in her hand this time.

Well, if nothing else, she sure is resourceful.

Only it wasn't necessary. Drake shook his head and the girl dropped it. It landed softly in the gravel, but it was enough to make the man turn.

"And who's this?"

Trust... you have to trust the man. You have no other choice.

Drake slipped the gun into the back of his pants.

"Hank, I'm in a bit of a bind here," Drake said, moving forward. He hooked a thumb at the container. "As you can probably tell."

Sgt. Henry Yasiv took another haul on his cigarette. The red ember illuminated his face, and Drake was startled to see how the man had aged. He looked at least a decade older than the last time they'd seen each other.

"I'd say," Yasiv said. He finished his cigarette and then immediately lit another. "I don't know if you watch the news, but DI Palmer is out to get your ass. I don't know what you did to piss him off, other than just being yourself, but he's *right* pissed. Except right now, he only wants you for questioning. At least, that's the official line. But now there's some chatter that he has some… incriminating… photos. I'm thinking that 'questioning' might soon be upgraded to 'wanted', especially with *this.*"

Yasiv pointed at the shipping container.

"No shit," Drake grumbled. He gestured for Mandy to come to his side. "This is Mandy—she's the girl I was telling you about."

Yasiv gave her a once over.

"I'm Sgt. Henry Yasiv," he said quietly. Mandy slid in behind Drake. "I'm going to—"

The sounds from the container to their right suddenly intensified.

"And that must be Officer Kramer."

Drake nodded.

"Can he hear us in there?"

Mandy shook her head.

"You can hear sounds, but not words. You can only hear words when the doors are open. That's when I heard about Drake."

Yasiv squinted at the girl before turning his attention to Drake.

"I can hold off DI Palmer for a while—not forever, but for a little while, no matter what photos he has. But this… Drake, Officer Kramer is an NYPD officer. Sure, he's an asshole, but you can't just brain a police officer over the head and lock him up."

Mandy stepped forward as if to correct the man, but Drake put a hand on her shoulder, effectively silencing the girl.

"I know. I know; I'll take the heat for that. But there is something more important that we have to deal with." Drake had already told Yasiv about the girls in the container over the phone and didn't feel the need to rehash it now. "There was a man here, a short man with gray hair, taking the bodies out to sea. I shot him in the hip, but it barely fazed him. I'm thinking the tough bastard was Bolivian or Russian or something like that. Likely with ties to organized crime. I know it's not much to go on, but we might get lucky if he was picked up recently in a drug trafficking sting, or something to do with the sex trade. Anything you can dig up might be able to help."

It was a shot in the dark, and both of the men knew it.

"I'll see what I can dig up," Yasiv said as he made his way to the front of the container. For a brief moment, Drake thought he was going to grab the tire iron and let Kramer out. But he stopped in front of it and then squatted on the blood covered gravel. Yasiv raised his eyes, and followed the trail of blood to the shore.

"What's that?" he asked.

Drake, not knowing what the man was referring to, shrugged.

Yasiv took the initiative and picked up a small square of paper and showed it to Drake. It looked like the upper right-hand corner of a business card of some sort. Drake took the card and rubbed a dot of blood off with his thumb.

"No clue," he said, thinking back to the shot that the Russian had taken in the hip.

Had it been in his pocket? It could've been…

"It looks like… I dunno, it looks like a leg of some sort," Yasiv said.

Drake nodded.

It really did look like the pale, slender leg of a woman ending in an expensive looking shoe.

Mandy suddenly appeared at Drake's side and looked at the image.

"They were handing those out in Colombia. A business card; *La chica con las piernas,* we called it. They said we would be working at a classy place here in America."

Drake chewed the inside of his lip and then slipped what was left of the business card into his pocket.

"Think you can give me a five-minute head start before you open the cage and let the wild animal out?"

Yasiv took the cigarette out of his mouth and looked at it.

"You have until I'm done with my smoke."

Drake nodded and turned to face Mandy.

"I want you to stay with Sgt. Yasiv. He's going to look after you for a little while, make sure you're safe."

Mandy opened her mouth to protest, but Drake shut her down before she could even get started.

"I'm going to find out who did this to you and your friends. That's a promise. But I can't do that if I'm always looking over my shoulder to make sure that you're okay. You need to promise me that you'll stay with Sgt. Yasiv. He's not like the others, he's a good man."

In his periphery, Drake saw Yasiv raise an eyebrow, but he ignored this. The fact that Yasiv had come here and put his career and maybe even his freedom on the line by speaking to him, was proof that he wasn't in bed with Ken Smith and the others.

Yasiv could be trusted… for now.

The man took a heavy drag of his smoke, and the white paper burned another quarter inch.

"I'll look after her, Drake. But you better get going."

With that, Drake spun and hurried back toward his car, clutching the right side of his body protectively.

He heard Mandy shout something, but he ignored her. Yasiv would keep her safe; he would do a much better job of it than Drake ever could, anyway.

After all, he was a shitty boyfriend, more than likely a terrible father, and he was a god-awful business partner—both on the force and as a PI.

But he was good at one thing. *Really* good at it.

Drake was good at catching bad guys. And the people who had done this… they weren't your run of the mill purse-snatchers.

These were murderers who had no shame, no morals, no code of ethics.

And they had to be stopped.

Chapter 24

DRAKE HAD ONLY JUST opened the door to Triple D when Screech ran toward him, eyes wide.

"You've got to see this, I think that—" he glanced behind Drake. "Wait... where's Mandy? I thought you said she was with you."

Drake stepped inside and closed the door behind him.

"She *was* with me," Drake confirmed. "But now she's with Sgt. Yasiv. He's going to look after her."

"He's not... you know, in the Mayor's pocket?"

Drake shrugged.

"I don't think so. I mean, if he was, he more than likely would've arrested me on the spot after what happened to officer Kramer."

Screech shook his head.

"I'm not even going to ask," he said, leading Drake to his desk.

Without another word, Screech pulled up a photograph surrounded by Spanish text. In it, Drake saw a younger looking Raul, but one with the same bristly mustache, the same flat features.

"It's Raul," he said mostly to himself.

"Sure is: *Raul Mendez*. But can you guess who has his arm on his shoulder?"

It was an American soldier, that much was clear by the fatigues that he wore. He had a shock of black hair and the beginnings of a beard on his tanned cheeks. The man looked familiar, but Drake couldn't place him.

"Look closer, look at his eyes," Screech instructed.

The man's pale blue irises were also familiar.

"Now picture him with the cigar in his mouth."

This was the trigger that Drake needed.

"No shit," he said. "That's Ken fucking Smith. That's the Mayor. Where is it taken from? When?"

"From Colombia, 1983 or 84, I can't tell for sure. You know what happened in 84 in Colombia?"

"Well, I was five so, no," Drake replied quickly. He kept studying the photograph as he listened to Screech talk; there was something about it that was a little off.

"Fair enough, I wasn't even born yet—but here's the thing: in 1984 the RAND Corporation was hired by the Department of Defense to look into whether or not military intervention would stem the shipment of cocaine from Colombia in the US."

"And let me guess, in an ironic twist, the RAND Corporation needed a military escort to conduct their study."

"Very good, my young squire. So, with this in mind, I want to introduce you to Lieut. Cpl. Ken Smith."

Drake nodded. He knew that Ken had served in the Army in the 80's. It had, after all, been a selling point for his campaign. After his stint in South America, Ken had returned and had enrolled in law school. The details from this period of Ken's life—from law school to founding Smith, Smith, and Jackson—were sketchy, but the consensus was that several shrewd investments and high-profile mergers had set him on his trajectory to become mayor.

"So, this is where and when he met Raul," Drake said, thinking out loud. "But what's this mumbo-jumbo Spanish shit all about?"

"Just wait."

Screech enlarged the image and focused his pointer on something behind the two men.

Drake leaned closer to the monitor. There appeared to be a sign just over Raul's left shoulder. The words were in Spanish, and they were cut off by the mens' faces, but there was a particular symbol that transcended language.

"A snake eating the eyeball," he muttered.

"And they say you're just a pretty face," Screech said. Upon seeing Drake's frown, he quickly continued. "Yeah, that's the same goddamn symbol that was on the drugs and matches the tattoo on Raul's arm. And that sign? The one that's cut off? It says the Church of… you guessed it, Liberation. I also managed to translate some of the article and the gist of it is that while the U.S. Army was helping the RAND Corporation they came across this church. Apparently, it was just a front for a drug lab. What's more, the people working in this drug lab had been kidnapped and written off as dead years beforehand. And guess who jumped in and saved the day? G.I. Ken, that's who."

Drake was sure to wrap his mind around everything that he'd just heard. He wasn't surprised about Raul's connection to Colombia, of course, or the drug trade. What was alarming was how deep Ken's ties appeared to run.

"So, Ken saves the day, liberates these people and then… what? Takes over the shop? Uses Raul to ship the drugs to the US? Forms ANGUIS holdings to cover everything up?"

Screech shrugged dramatically.

"Your guess is as good as mine… but I'm thinking it's a pretty good guess. I tried to find if there was anything about this whole Church of Liberation in US papers, and only found one small article about it. No names were used, only the mention of the Church and how it had been… uh… *liberated*. It appeared in the Times about six months after it happened."

Drake scratched his head. Mandy was from Colombia, so it wouldn't be a stretch to think that Ken was somehow behind what had happened to these girls. The drugs, the logo, the tattoo on Raul's arm: they all depicted a snake eating an eyeball.

It was definitely connected.

And then there was the matter of the woman's leg on the business card that he'd blasted out of some Russian midget's pocket. There was that, too.

"Good stuff; keep digging, Screech. Anything we can—wait did you say the *Times*?"

Screech nodded and pulled up another newspaper article.

"Yep, the Times."

"And let me guess who the author is: Ivan Meitzer."

Screech clicked his mouse until a byline appeared on screen. The article was indeed written by Ivan Meitzer.

Drake's thoughts turned back to the day in the hangar when Meitzer had been beaten by Raul to get him to stop posting articles about Drake's activities.

It appeared as if their relationship went back a ways, too.

Drake pulled the business card out of his pocket and held it out to Screech. The man noticed the blood on the corner and raised an eyebrow.

"I'm not gonna ask about that, either. What's this card all about?"

"I think… I think this is where Mandy and the girls were headed in New York. I'm guessing it's a gentleman's club of sorts. What I do know for sure, is that if Ken is behind this, he won't be happy that his girls are dead. I also bet that he's going to try to bring more into the city."

Screech's face suddenly grew dark.

"If they survive the journey overseas, that is."

"Shit," Drake grumbled. He leaned back and rubbed his side absently. "And now that his drop point is compromised he's going to be looking for another. Another location that is owned by ANGUIS."

"One of about a hundred and fifty."

This sobering thought brought about silence that lasted a full minute before Drake pulled an about-face.

"What about the other thing I asked you about? The people behind ANGUIS? Anything on that front?"

Screech pulled up another document.

"You're in luck. I managed to trace recent money sent from ANGUIS to four accounts. None linked back to Ken, unfortunately, but there is a Russian name on the list."

"Boris Brackovich," Drake read out loud. Unlike the other information that Screech had provided, however interesting, this was something he might be able to act upon. "Get me a printout and send one to Yasiv. See what he can dig up on this Boris guy."

Chapter 25

BECKETT CLOSED THE DOOR to the mass spec machine and watched the mechanical arm take the sample inside. As he waited for the readout, his mind turned to what had happened on the yacht. He had tried to push these images from his mind, but no matter what he did, they kept coming back.

Despite what he'd said, Screech was right; it *was* all related. It *had* to be.

And Beckett wasn't naïve; he knew that Bob Bumacher intended to use the yacht to smuggle the drugs that were on board. Hell, he was fairly certain that the yacht had actually belonged to Donnie DiMarco.

That didn't change the fact that DiMarco deserved to die. Bob on the other hand… up until this point, he hadn't killed anybody, at least not to Beckett's knowledge.

Now, however, after hearing about what had happened to the girls, Beckett was beginning to think that Bob didn't deserve his free pass.

The machine beeped and produced a readout, drawing him out of his head. Beckett took a quick look at the screen and then whistled.

"Well slap my ass and call me Sally," he said under his breath.

The heroin was of Colombian origin and was almost laboratory grade shit; ninety-five percent pure, cut with…

Beckett didn't recognize the second, much smaller peak, and used the embedded software to search for a comparison. It took all of thirty seconds to come back with a match.

C22H28N2O.

Fentanyl.

The package of heroin that Screech had given him weighed exactly 100g. Even if the girls had swallowed just a teaspoon of that shit, the fentanyl would likely kill them. And they hadn't swallowed a teaspoon, they'd swallowed *twenty* bags.

No, Beckett concluded, Bob Bumacher was not a good man.

Upon closer inspection, he realized that there were also trace amounts of other substances. He ran a comparison on these, and when the results pinged he didn't whistle this time. He cringed.

In addition to the fentanyl, the heroin was also laced with Carfentanyl—an elephant tranquilizer—as well as two even more powerful variants: Ohmefentanyl and Lofentanil. Just a single grain of either of these would mean almost certain death.

"Fuck."

The last thing Beckett wanted to do right now was to get involved with Drake and Screech and Bob Bumacher. His finger still ached, and his mind was a scrambled mess.

And the nightmares…

As he stared at the screen, Beckett found himself absently rubbing the tattoos under his right armpit, the three lines that represented Craig Sloan, Donnie DiMarco, and Ray Reynolds.

He didn't want to get involved, but after seeing what they were trying to bring into New York, what choice did he have?

Chapter 26

"GODDAMN IT," SCREECH SWORE, bringing a fist down on the table.

Drake startled and opened his eyes. He must've fallen asleep at Screech's desk, although he couldn't remember doing so. A quick check of his watch told him that it was coming on three in the morning.

"What?" he asked in a groggy voice. "What did you find?"

Screech shook his head.

"It's not what I found, it's what I *didn't* find." He pointed at the image onscreen which depicted the same leg, this time with a matching second one, that Drake had found on the card at the hangar. "You were right—it appears that this is from a private gentleman's club. But this isn't your local rippers. This is real cloak and dagger shit. I can't find out who the girls are, where the place is, nothing. It's so secretive, I'd need all the computer power of NASA to break in."

Drake was disappointed, but he wasn't surprised.

Screech typed something into the password box, but it simply vibrated and notified him that it was incorrect.

"Shit," Screech muttered. "I give up. I'm not getting there. And unless you have connections with some high-priced hookers, then you're not getting there either. I think our best bet at this point is to narrow down the most likely locations for the shipment drop and hope we get lucky."

Drake frowned. That wasn't a plan, that was a guess.

And Drake didn't like guessing. He liked hard facts.

There has to be a way…

Screech's words suddenly echoed in his head.

Unless you have connections with some high-priced hookers…

Drake rubbed his chin.

"You know what? I might just know someone who might be able to get us in the door."

Screech looked at him with a raised eyebrow.

"You sly dog, you. Who would've thunk it."

Drake ignored the comment.

"I'm pretty sure that I know someone who might be able to help. It's just a matter of using the right method of persuasion."

***

Drake tapped the yellow envelope in his palm.

"Should I ask where you got this from?"

Screech shook his head.

"But you're okay to part with it?"

"I wouldn't worry about it. I'm more concerned about how you know about a place like this and why you think that a prostitute working in this neighborhood might be able to help us out."

Drake almost chuckled. He'd thought the same thing the first time he came here.

"It's a long story from back when I was a Detective. Anyways, this girl can be pretty feisty so if I'm not down in 20 minutes, get the fuck out of here," Drake said as he stepped out into the night.

It was almost four in the morning now, but something told him that the woman he was visiting would still be up—some professions never slept.

The real question was whether or not she would open the door for him.

Drake opened the rundown outer door to the apartment complex and then walked over to the intercom system.

"Here goes nothing," he muttered as he pressed the button marked only with a *V*.

A moment later, a female voice answered.

"*V*."

Drake cleared his throat.

"It's Raul," he said and then cringed. He had meant to put on his best Spanish accent, but somehow it had come out sounding Irish.

But to his surprise, there was a buzzing sound and Drake pulled the inner door open. Once inside, he was brought back to an earlier time, a much different time when he had still been part of the NYPD. His eyes turned to the hallway that he had once laid in, pretending to be a heroin addict when Raul walked by him.

Drake shook his head. That time was long past.

He hurried upstairs, making his way down the hall to the door that was painted to look like all the others, but one he knew from experience was made of reinforced steel.

He was about to knock when it suddenly sprung open and a petite woman in a nightgown leaped out. Drake was so taken by surprise that he stumbled backward.

Then he heard the crackle of a Taser.

"You again," Veronica said. "I swear, you men never learn."

Chapter 27

SCREECH SQUINTED AT THE dilapidated apartment building and wondered if this was going to lead anywhere. Part of him wanted to call Yasiv, to find out if Mandy was still okay, while another part of him couldn't get her naked body out of his mind.

Back in the Virgin Gorda, he'd seen some pretty amazing looking women—some of the most beautiful women that he'd ever laid eyes on either live or in film. But Mandy… she was different, somehow. She *was* beautiful, sure, but she was also real in a way that the girls on *B-Yacht'ch* weren't.

Another part of him thought that Drake had just lost his fucking mind, that everything that had happened to him at the Reynolds farm had finally gotten to his head.

That the demons who haunted him had finally won.

He was fiddling with his phone when it buzzed in his hand and he answered without even looking at the caller.

"Screech here."

"It's Beckett. I ran your powder… it came back almost pure. But it wasn't cut with baking powder or laxatives. It was cut with fentanyl and other, more deadly variants."

Screech's eyes widened. Heroin was dangerous enough, but fentanyl? A single dose could kill you.

It seemed counterintuitive to lace your product with something as deadly as fentanyl, but it was in high demand. The sad fact was, the more risk involved, the more addicts wanted it.

His brother had taught him that.

"Which is why the girls died when the plastic bags dissolved in their stomachs," Beckett continued. "As for the other thing? The bodies? Nothing that matches your description came through the morgue."

Screech nodded to himself.

"Long story, but those bodies have been disposed of," he said absently, trying not to picture Mandy lying on the ground, foam at the corners of her dead lips.

"Disposed of?" Beckett asked, the octave of his voice rising.

"Some Russian guy… Drake winged him with a bullet, but he still managed to take all the bodies out to sea. I'm guessing that they're at the bottom of the Pacific Ocean by now."

There was an awkward pause that went on for so long that Screech thought that Beckett had hung up on him.

"You still there?"

"Yeah, I'm still here. Listen, I may have changed my mind about this. I think I'm going to lend a hand, look into how these girls made it from Colombia all the way to New York."

Screech chewed the inside of his cheek. Even though he had gone to the man for help, he wasn't sure he was keen on Beckett getting involved.

When Beckett got involved, people ended up dead.

As these thoughts ran through Screech's head, he glanced up at the rearview mirror only to see his face staring back.

"Screech?"

"Yeah, look, Beckett, I don't know if it's the best—"

"I can do things that Drake can't," Beckett said sharply. "I can go to places he's not willing to go."

Screech cleared his throat. He felt guilty for not doing anything about the dope on the yacht, and he wanted nothing more than to extract revenge for what happened to Mandy and the other girls. But this… did anyone deserve what Beckett was proposing?

"That's what I was afraid of," he said glumly.

Chapter 28

"I'M ONLY HERE TO ask you a few questions, that's it. Now please, put the Taser down."

Veronica sneered.

"Last time you came here, you dragged my ass out in handcuffs wearing a Frozen nightie. Paraded me around like I was a… well, you know."

Veronica crackled the Taser as she spoke, and Drake continued to step backward toward the stairs. His eyes darted from her angry face to the angrier Taser leads.

"Look, I'm not even a cop anymore. I haven't been a cop for a long time now. In fact, I'm actually wanted by the cops."

Veronica's brow furrowed.

"Maybe I should give them a call then, tell them to come pick your ass up. Add harassment to whatever charges they want you for."

Drake started to reach behind him for the envelope that Screech had handed him in the car.

"Don't even think about it," Veronica snapped, leading with the Taser.

Drake had been tased twice prior in his life: once by accident by a rookie police officer and the other by a drug dealer who'd gotten the jump on him. These incidents had been some of the most excruciating of his life. It felt as if his entire body was on fire, but instead of stopping, dropping, and rolling, the only thing he could do was clench his jaw together. In fact, his body had seized, and his brain felt as if someone had dumped kerosene in one ear and tossed a lit flare into the other.

Drake never wanted to feel that sort of pain again. It made his current torment feel like a hangnail by comparison.

"I've got a package for you, Veronica. Cash."

"I don't need your money."

Drake started to turn.

"You may not need it, but I bet you want it. I remember Raul coming to you with one just like this. And unlike what he asked of you, all I have are a few questions."

Drake untucked his shirt, showing Veronica that the only thing he was carrying was the envelope.

"Turn around slowly, Drake," she instructed.

She remembers my name; that's something, at least.

When he had his back to her, Drake heard the crackle of the Taser and prepared himself as best he could for what was to come. But the tasing never came. Instead, he felt the envelope being yanked from the back of his pants.

"Can I turn around now?" he asked, hands still in the air.

"Slowly."

Veronica still held the Taser in one hand, but used the other to open the envelope. Drake knew that the moment she saw the cash and started to do some mental math, he'd have a shot to wrench the Taser from her. Veronica was petite, but she was feisty, and he knew that if he didn't take this opportunity now, he probably wouldn't get another.

But he did nothing; he wasn't here to start a fight. Drake was here for information, something that required her cooperation.

"It's a little light," Veronica said as she closed the envelope.

Drake shrugged.

"It's also four in the morning and it's all I could get. It may be light, but it's plenty just to answer a few questions."

Veronica pressed her full lips together as she contemplated this. Eventually, she tilted her head toward the door.

"A few questions, that's it. And that's only because you caught the bastard who killed Tom Smith."

Drake's memory flashed back to when he'd apprehended Dr. Mark Kruk, followed by his most recent meeting with the man in the psychiatric facility. Something told him that these interactions with the doctor with the split personality weren't going to be his last.

Hands still raised, he walked slowly into the apartment. Veronica followed him inside and locked the door behind them.

The room hadn't changed much since he'd been here about a year ago. There was a large bed on one side of the room with four massive posts that extended to the ceiling, and there was a makeup stand to the right. The only new addition, so far as he could tell, was on one wall: hanging from a pegboard was an array of sexual devices, everything from a paddle, to a two-headed black dildo approximately the size of a Louisville slugger, and numerous other things that Drake couldn't even imagine uses for.

"Sit on the corner of the bed," she instructed. Drake did as he was told. Despite the fact that the room smelled faintly of lavender and was meticulously clean, he was still apprehensive about sitting on the bed given Veronica's profession. But his discomfort played second fiddle to his fear of being tased. "Now, what do you want to know?"

Drake started to reach into the pocket of his jeans when Veronica leaned forward with the Taser.

"I'm just getting a piece of paper. Jesus, relax."

"People in my profession who relax contract chlamydia or end up dead."

Good point, Drake thought.

He took out a piece of paper that Screech had printed from the Internet. It was a blown-up version of the icon on the business card: two female legs that ended in lacy shoes.

"Have you ever seen this before," he said, tossing the paper at the woman. Veronica kept her eyes locked on Drake as she unfolded it.

"I hope this is worth ten grand to you, because—" she stopped speaking the second her eyes darted at the paper. "Where did you get this? Where the hell did you get this?"

Chapter 29

IT'S AMAZING WHAT YOU can find online these days, Beckett thought with a smirk. He would have thought that a man like Bob Bumacher, given his profession—which was looking more and more like it consisted of mainly smuggling women and drugs—would have exercised some discretion when it came to posting online.

As it turned out, a simple Internet search revealed not only Bob's address, but his phone number as well.

Beckett checked his watch. Normal people were sleeping at this hour.

But he wasn't normal.

He hadn't been normal since that day he'd come across Craig down the side of the burning house.

After printing out Bob's Manhattan address, Beckett pulled a leather case out of his desk. Inside, he laid a scalpel, a syringe loaded with Midazolam, and then, after a moment's contemplation, he threw in the bag of heroin that Screech had given him.

Satisfied, he stood and stretched his back. It had been a long day—shit, it had been a long week, and it wasn't about to end. Not just yet, anyway.

With a sigh, he made his way toward the door and peered back into his room one last time. Beckett knew that the risk of what he planned to do was even greater than when he'd dealt with Craig Sloan and Donnie DiMarco. Craig had been a known murderer and it had been easy to claim self-defense. Donnie had died on foreign land run by corrupt cops that had been paid off on his behalf.

But Bob Bumacher—according to his 'official' profile at least—was a well-liked fitness trainer that would most definitely be missed. And a man of his immense size would pose a physical challenge as well.

And yet, if Beckett found concrete proof that Bob knew about the girls, that he was responsible for bringing them over from Colombia, then he had to pay.

Drake had his methods, his connections in the police force, his analytical process.

Beckett, on the other hand, had a more rudimentary approach. An ancient one, but crude none-the-less.

With a self-assured nod, he tucked the small leather case into his pocket and left his apartment.

If Bob is responsible in any way for what happened to those girls, he will pay.

Chapter 30

"THAT... THAT'S A LONG story," Drake said apprehensively. Veronica's visceral reaction to the image on the page had been startling, to say the least. "I just want to know if you've heard of these guys, if you know where I can find them."

Veronica shook her head.

"You don't want anything to do with these guys, Drake. Trust me on that one."

Drake frowned.

"Is it a strip club? Escort service?"

Veronica shook her head.

"No."

Drake threw his arms up in frustration.

"I gave you the money, and you said you'd answer my questions. But you aren't giving me shit? Who are these guys? What the fuck is this thing?"

Veronica's eyes narrowed and for the first time since Drake appeared at her door, she lowered the Taser to her lap.

"It's not an escort service, Drake. It's an auction."

Drake's jaw went slack.

"An auction? They're *selling* these girls?"

Veronica nodded and set the Taser down on the chair beside her. She took a deep breath, then finally started opening up.

"Before I started here, myself and a couple other street workers were approached by a man with this symbol on a business card. You see, Drake, on the street, every girl is your competition, but every girl is also your safety net. If something goes wrong, if a John goes too far or tries to get something he didn't pay for, the best protection you have isn't you guys—the police—but your fellow street worker. There's power in numbers, Drake. But you need to earn the respect of your fellow workers before they'll put their neck on the line for you.

"There was this one girl, a young girl who had just come up from somewhere in the South, one of the Carolinas I believe, and she was as green as they come. Nancy, I think her name was. Anyways, on her first trick, she forgot to get the money upfront then didn't get paid at all. Her second trick was even worse: the John choked her so bad that she had to wear a scarf in the middle of August to cover up the bruises. I tried to help her out, give her tips, but it was clear she wasn't cut out for this job. So, when the man with the card approached us and asked about whether or not we wanted something safer, something more secure, Nancy jumped at the opportunity. Usually, this is the same shit that pimps tell you, but this man… he was different. He was no pimp, at least not in the traditional sense.

"When you've been in the game for as long as I have, you just get feelings about people. And I felt that this was a very bad man. I tried to convince Nancy not to go with him, but she was naive and scared. That was the last time I saw her alive," Veronica paused for a moment to catch her breath. "About a month later, one of the other workers found her body in a dumpster on 42nd Ave. Her throat had been slit ear to ear, but this was probably a mercy killing. Her body… Drake, it had been ravaged. I can't even—just thinking about it now makes me want to cry or puke or something."

Veronica handed the print out back to Drake. Her hand was shaking so badly that it fluttered.

"You don't want to fuck with these guys, Drake. I hear that they're mobbed up, but we're not talking about Mafia. We're talking about Colombians, cartels, that kind of shit."

Drake thought back to the gray-haired man outside the hanger.

"Russians?"

Veronica shrugged.

"Who knows. These guys, these scumbags, they often work together."

"But these people… the ones that would *buy* these girls. What kind of person would do that?"

Veronica chewed her lip and took a moment before answering. It was clear that she was remembering something from her own past.

"What happens to a person when their entire self-worth is wrapped up in the things they can buy? What happens when they've already bought everything? New experiences don't exist for these rich assholes. You know how it is, Drake. For these people, it's not about money, it never was; money is simply a tool to gain power. After all, they don't call it *buy anything* money," she shook her head. "No, they call it *fuck you* money. When you have this much money, you can tell anyone you want to fuck off. They say it all the time to people like you and me, the police, the FBI, anybody, really."

Drake struggled to take all of this in. He wasn't naïve, and he doubted the girls in the container were either. They were coming to New York to ply the sex trade, that much was obvious. But Mandy didn't mention anything about being *sold*. Clearly, that was part of the fine print that they hadn't been privy to.

He cleared his throat.

"Well, you see, Veronica, here's the thing. I don't give a fuck about the FBI or NYPD, either. What I give a fuck about is the fact that two dozen girls were found dead in a shipping container. They died because whoever was bringing them in from Colombia decided it would be a good idea to pack them so full of heroin that the baggies burst in their stomachs. Two birds and one stone, that sort of shit. That's what I care about. I don't give a fuck about mobsters or rich assholes. All I care about is making sure that what I saw in that container doesn't happen again. That none of your friends are ever found in dumpsters with their throats slit. That's what *I* care about. But I can't do it on my own. I've got very few friends left, but even with their skills, they can't find out where these assholes are hiding. That's what I need you for."

Drake leaned forward and interlaced his fingers.

"You think you can help me out, Veronica? Can you help me find these assholes and finally be the one to tell *them* to fuck off?"

Chapter 31

BECKETT STARED UP AT Bob Bumacher's house through the windshield. It was a three-story brownstone that must've cost at least seven figures. Expensive digs for a personal trainer.

He slipped the leather case out of his pocket and rechecked the contents.

I should just go home and get some sleep, he thought unexpectedly. *When I wake up, I'll call the police, let them know what Bob's been up to. Let them deal with it.*

But something inside of Beckett had awoken. Something that gripped him, something that had a stranglehold on his soul.

No, Bob Bumacher has to pay.

And Beckett was the one who had come to collect his debt.

With a deep breath, Beckett's eyes flicked up to the rearview mirror. He caught his reflection and was momentarily startled. It wasn't his face that was shocking, even though he looked older and more tired than he remembered.

It was his eyes—there was an emptiness to his eyes that was alarming.

Following another deep breath, Beckett stepped out into the night. He went to the trunk first and put on two pairs of purple lab gloves before slipping a balaclava over his head and face. In addition to these items, he'd also picked up several rudimentary lock picking tools: a baseball bat and a crowbar. He opted for the latter.

He walked briskly down the side of the house, looking for a way in. After about ten paces, he found it in the form of a window roughly six feet up. Hoisting himself up wouldn't be a problem, but it would prove difficult to pry the window open from below without making a racket. Glancing around, he found a recycling bin against the wall and wheeled it over. He placed it beneath the window and, after confirming that it would hold his weight, climbed on top of it.

A quick glance inside the house revealed that the window led into the kitchen. Beckett jammed the crowbar between the window and frame and it popped open with ease.

It probably hadn't even been locked.

After waiting to make sure that there was no stirring within the dark house, he put the crowbar on the counter inside and then hoisted himself through the opening.

Once inside, he paused again and listened closely.

Nothing, no sound. Not even an AC unit.

He climbed off the counter and looked around, trying to orient himself. The kitchen, which looked as if it had been taken straight out of a Home and Garden magazine, led to a family room off to the right and the entrance to the left. There was a staircase across to the entrance.

Even though he was sure that Bob was upstairs sleeping, Beckett went to the family room first.

He still needed proof that Bob was involved with the dead girls. The heroin, the yacht in the Virgin Gorda, the corrupt cops he'd paid off, they weren't enough.

The problem was, Beckett had no idea what he was looking for. It wasn't like the man would have pictures of himself posing with the dead bodies on display. He'd spent some time with Bob on the yacht when he'd ferried Beckett and Screech to the mainland, and while Bob didn't strike him as an intellectual, he wasn't an absolute moron, either.

A desk, maybe? Files? Computers?

When the family room gave him nothing but a flat-screen TV and a glass coffee table, Beckett started to question what he was doing here.

I should have found proof first, then come in. I should have planned this better.

Just when he was considering going back out the way he'd come, he spotted a door that he had overlooked at first. It was partially blocked by the TV, but there was more than enough room for him to slip behind it. When he saw the electronic keypad above an industrial looking doorknob, he couldn't help but smirk.

If Bob had anything incriminating in this house, it would be in this room.

But Beckett quickly realized that he had a new problem: while the window had popped open without much effort, this door was clearly reinforced. And no matter how hard he pushed the crowbar, it wouldn't budge.

Sweat forming beneath the balaclava, Beckett ground his teeth in frustration.

This is never going to work. It's solid steel.

Taking a step back, he reassessed his options. The crowbar wouldn't work, but maybe the keypad would.

After unsuccessfully trying a few number combinations, he simply grabbed the face of the thing and pulled. It came free in his hand, revealing just two wires that extended into the door itself. Beckett tore the pad off completely, then, on a whim, he touched the ends of the two wires together. There was a click and the door swung open.

You can buy the most expensive lock in the world, but if you installed it, there's always going to be a way to remove it.

Beckett stepped into the room and took a moment to catch his bearings. There were several shotguns mounted on the wall on his left and a tactical vest that hung beside them.

"You've been busy, Bob. Preparing for battle, are we?" he whispered. To his right was a computer as well as a filing cabinet. But Beckett didn't need to go rooting through any files to find what he was looking for.

Sitting on top of the computer desk was a set of keys attached to a floating device—the keys to *B-yacht'ch.* Beckett strode over and moved the keys aside. There, beneath the keys, was a manifest outlining travel plans from Manhattan to the shores of Colombia, with a stop in the Virgin Gorda. It was scheduled to leave that evening.

This was all the proof Beckett needed.

Bob knew about the girls, alright. He knew, because he'd transported them in the yacht.

"You've been a bad—"

Beckett's entire body froze when a voice spoke from behind him.

"What the fuck do you think you're doing?

Chapter 32

"WHO THE HELL IS this?" Screech demanded from the passenger seat of Drake's Crown Vic.

"Long story," Drake replied as he slid in behind the steering wheel. Veronica got into the back.

Screech's eyes darted from Drake to Veronica and back again.

"What the fuck, Drake? What's going on?"

Drake started the car and put it into drive.

"Veronica, this is Screech—he's my partner."

"Doesn't seem like your type," Veronica said from the backseat.

"Sorry, sweetheart, forgot to shave my legs this morning," Screech shot back. Drake's eyes flicked to the rearview, and he saw that Veronica had removed the Taser from her purse.

"Fuck off, both of you. Screech, Veronica's gonna help us figure out when and how we can get into the next auction."

"Auction?"

Drake nodded.

"The card I found… it's not from a gentlemen's club. It's an auction where they sell these Colombian girls as sex slaves."

In his periphery, Drake saw Screech cringe. He didn't blame the man. Drake himself felt sick to his stomach just thinking about what could have happened to those girls. And as cruel as it sounded, after what Veronica had told him, it might have been a blessing that the girls in the container had gone out the way they did.

And if these thoughts made Drake uneasy, a hardened ex-NYPD detective, what might they do to the mind of a computer analyst?

Drake suddenly pulled over to the side of the road quickly and jammed the car into park. Then he turned his entire body to face Screech.

"Screech, I can take you home. I can take you home, and you never have to hear about this again. You don't have to be involved—and you won't have to worry about Mandy. I promise that I'll look after her. But you don't have to do this, you've got nothing to prove... not to me, not to Beckett, not to anyone. What you've done for me is already more than anyone could ask."

Screech's face twisted and he cast a glance in the backseat.

"Forget about Veronica—she can take care of herself. Trust me on that one. This is just about you now. Just say the word and I'll take you home."

Screech seemed to contemplate this for a few moments, but when he was going to do just that—ask Drake to take him home—he did an about-face.

"I spoke to Beckett," he said softly. "He told me that the heroin that Mandy had was laced with fentanyl and some other, even more powerful stuff. He said it's the most dangerous shit he's ever come across. And this is the senior ME of the NYPD we're talking about here."

Drake nodded; that was answer enough for him. He put the car into drive and continued onward.

Less than a half an hour later, Veronica and Screech had warmed to each other. Drake wasn't surprised; both of them had a crude sense of humor, and it was mildly amusing to listen to their back and forth banter. But most of the time, his mind was preoccupied. Somehow Beckett was back in the fold, as was Screech, and now he had brought Veronica along for the ride as well.

It seemed that no matter how hard Drake tried to stay out of people's business, to keep his misery to himself, it was like a disease that spread from one capillary to another.

He tried to convince himself that they were doing good, that the whole point of everything they were up to revolved around making the city safe, but he couldn't help but think that it was also centered around one incident.

Clay.

"Here's good."

Clay and the Skeleton King, the fact that his best friend and partner had been murdered in front of his eyes.

Due to his negligence.

"Drake, I said, here's good."

Why did you have to go and get yourself mixed up in this shit, Clay? ANGUIS Holdings? The Church of Liberation?

And he couldn't forget about the image of Jasmine holding the brick of heroin.

Why didn't you just stay out of all that garbage? And why didn't you just talk to me? Why didn't—

"Drake! Let me out of the fucking car!"

Drake shook his head and turned to look at Veronica.

"Fuck, I've been asking you to let me out for the past five minutes."

Drake pulled over to the side of the road. He hadn't even realized that they'd already arrived in the heart of Manhattan, so lost in his head was he.

"Here?"

"No, back there, when I first asked you to stop." Veronica sighed. "Never mind, here's fine."

Drake looked around. The street was nearly empty, which wasn't surprising given the hour. And yet, he spotted a woman in a miniskirt and tube top slowly sauntering toward their parked car, a cigarette dangling between her lips.

"Are you sure—"

"Look, these assholes aren't just going to advertise their auction on a plaque or on a banner behind a plane. Let me work the streets for a while. If what you said is true, they're going to be desperate for more girls now that their shipment…" she let her sentence trail off. "One night, maybe two—I'll figure out when the auction is going down."

Drake nodded.

"You want us to… I dunno, wait around? Watch out for you?"

Veronica rolled her eyes in the backseat and got out of the car. Then she walked over to Drake's half-open window.

"This is all the protection I need," she said, flashing him the Taser.

Just seeing that weapon again made Drake shudder.

Yeah, Veronica could most definitely look after herself.

Chapter 33

In person, Bob Bumacher was gigantic. For the brief second that Beckett had to observe the man before he lunged, a strange thought entered his head.

The white hulk—he looks like the white hulk.

Despite his shock, Beckett somehow managed to swivel his hips a second before the man's massive hands grabbed him, something that more than likely saved his life.

Instead of striking him directly in the chest, Bob hit Beckett's left shoulder, sending him spiraling towards the desk. A second later, his hip banged against the filing cabinet, and he cried out in pain.

The momentum sent Bob spinning in the other direction and he collided loudly with the wall. Knowing that he just had a few seconds before the big man recovered, Beckett reached for the crowbar that he had set down on the desk upon entering the room.

Only it wasn't there. When his hip had struck the table, it must have fallen to the floor, he realized. Beckett quickly dropped to his knees to search for it. It had slipped behind the desk and was now lying near the back wall, but as he reached for it, a vice grip closed on his left ankle.

"No!" Beckett yelled.

Bob Bumacher took this as encouragement and yanked. *Hard.*

For a moment, Beckett was airborne, but this only lasted a split second before he crashed into the opposite wall.

Bob was on his feet again, snarling now, the veins in his bare chest and arms and even his head throbbing.

He truly was the white hulk.

Beckett collapsed to the floor, pain shooting up his left hip and ankle.

"I can—" *explain,* he tried to say. But Bob came for him again, throwing a punch at his head. Survival instincts took over and Beckett somehow managed to roll to one side to avoid the blow.

Bob's fist blasted a hole in the drywall the size of a beach ball.

This was a terrible fucking plan, Beckett thought absently. Still on the floor, he looked at the crowbar again, but now that he was on the other side of the room, he knew that there was no way to reach it before Bob tore his limbs from his body.

A sharp pain shot up his hip, and it took him a moment to realize that it wasn't just from striking the desk, but that there was something hard in there.

Your case! The Midazolam! The scalpel, you fucking idiot!

"You made a mistake coming here," Bob hissed.

Beckett rolled onto his back just in time to see Bob jump on top of him. Before he could react, the man was in full mount, putting his weight, which must've been in excess of 280 pounds, directly on Beckett's chest. He couldn't draw a breath, he couldn't even so much as wheeze.

Beckett was a brown belt in jiu-jitsu, but he was terribly outmatched in this situation.

"I'm going to enjoy killing you," Bob said, his eyes blazing.

All it would take was one solid punch to the head and Beckett knew that his skull would collapse like a paper mache piñata. Thankfully, Bob had different ideas.

He reached down with both hands and slowly wrapped them around Beckett's throat.

"Yeah, I'm really gonna enjoy this."

As the man started to squeeze, Beckett used the hand not to try to fend the man off—an impossible task in the best of circumstances—to retrieve the case from his pocket. As the pressure on his throat increased, Beckett felt his airway start to close and spots started to speckle his vision.

And yet, he somehow managed to pull the case out. Next, he slipped a finger beneath the zipper and slid it open. Then he reached inside.

"I don't know who the fuck you are, but you messed with the wrong fucking dude," Bob said with a grin.

As his tunnel vision started to increase, Beckett struggled to grab the syringe from within the case. His fingers kept slipping, though, owing mostly to the fact that he was missing one of them.

"Beckkkk—" he struggled to say, but his voice was only a wet whisper.

"I don't care if you beg for your life, you're a dead man," Bob snapped back.

"Beckkkkkk—" Beckett tried again, but failed.

Beckett's hand finally closed on the syringe, and he awkwardly put two fingers—the first and third—behind the finger guards and placed his thumb on the plunger. Then, with the last bit of strength he possessed, Beckett squeezed his neck muscles as tightly as possible to give himself just enough room to utter a single word.

"Beckettt!"

This time, Bob seemed to understand. He used one hand to grab Beckett's balaclava and tear it off his head. The cold look in his eyes suddenly became one of confusion.

"Beckett?" He repeated. With only one hand around his throat now, blood flooded Beckett's brain and charged him with adrenaline.

He jammed the syringe in the man's biceps. He got lucky and hit one of the several bulging veins, and somehow managed to inject the entire dose of Midazolam directly into Bob's circulatory system.

But Midazolam wasn't instant, even injected intravenously, and Beckett knew that it would take a few minutes to act. He'd also pegged Bob at only 240 pounds, give or take—the man weighed much more than that. To top it off, it wasn't supposed to kill the man, only incapacitate him.

All of these things worked against Beckett.

But what the drug did serve to do, was distract the man further. Bob leaned back from Beckett's chest and turned to look at his own arm. Even though Bob's free hand was still around Beckett's throat, it was now loose enough that he could draw a full breath.

"Did… did Ken send you?" he grumbled, a confused look on his face.

And this was the other distraction that Beckett needed. He'd since dropped the syringe, and now reached back into the case and pulled out the scalpel.

"What are you—"

Beckett didn't hesitate. He buried the scalpel blade in the man's neck. Bob seemed surprised by this more than anything, and Beckett withdrew the blade and jabbed it a second time.

He managed to strike the man seven or eight times in rapid succession, all in and around the left side of his neck, hoping desperately to hit his carotid artery.

And, judging by the sheer volume of blood that started to spray down, Beckett was pretty sure he'd succeeded.

The entire time he stabbed Bob, Beckett tried to buck the man off him. But Bob was just too big and too strong. Even as blood soaked Beckett's face and chest, Bob still looked down at him with a confused expression on his face.

By the dozenth blow, the ragged hole was so large that air started to hiss out of Bob like a punctured inner tube.

Eventually, Bob Bumacher's limp body collapsed on top of Beckett. It took all of Beckett's remaining strength to roll the big man off him. For nearly a full minute, Beckett struggled to take a full breath, to clear the spots that clouded his vision. As he stared up at the ceiling, blood from the dying man continued to soak his entire body.

He must have laid there for five, maybe ten minutes before he heard the sound of the door opening.

Beckett, still dizzy from the lack of oxygen, somehow managed to scramble on to all fours, his hand instinctively tightening on the scalpel that was still clutched between his fingers.

He expected to be confronted by one of Bob's gym buddies, a roommate, maybe even his wife.

Or a cop who had been called to the scene due to all the noise.

But when he finally saw who it was, his entire body went cold.

It was a young boy of maybe four or five years, dressed in white flannel pajamas. He clutched a Teddy bear in one hand, while the other was jammed into his mouth.

Beckett grabbed the side of the desk and managed to haul himself to his feet. Then he grabbed the manifest from beneath the yacht keys, tossed the bag of heroin that he had brought with him onto the floor, and stumbled out of the room.

The entire time, he muttered, *I'm sorry*, over and over and over again in a dry whisper.

Chapter 34

DRAKE PULLED INTO THE parking lot of Triple D just as the sun kissed the horizon. As if on cue, Screech yawned and a moment later, Drake followed suit.

"What now?" Screech asked after his jaw slammed shut. Drake looked at his partner and marveled at how bloodshot his eyes were.

He couldn't even imagine what his own looked like.

"Now, I think we should get some sleep."

Screech squinted.

"Do you ever sleep?"

It was a simple question, and likely even rhetorical, but it gave Drake pause. The truth was, he didn't sleep—not really. He passed out; that was the only way to ensure he didn't have nightmares.

Nightmares that featured the skeletal version of Clay.

"Not really," he admitted at last.

Screech turned his eyes to the strip mall that housed Triple D Investigations until his gaze eventually fixated on the worn wooden door.

"Then what the hell are we doing here? Shit, this is the first place that DI Palmer would look for you. In fact, I'm surprised that he isn't here now, waiting to arrest your ass."

The man had a point.

What *was* he doing here?

He should be home with Jasmine trying to smooth things over, making her comfortable.

But that would make him a sitting duck for Palmer. As for friends that he might crash with? Screech and Beckett were the only two people who even came close to fitting that description, but they were both out of the question. The cops had already been to Screech's place, and even though Beckett now seemed more amenable to getting involved with the dead Colombian girls, their last interaction had been less than cordial.

"I have nowhere else to go," Drake admitted with a shrug.

But that wasn't entirely true; there was still family to consider. With all of the craziness of the last forty-eight hours, he'd nearly forgotten about his brother who had come out of the woodwork at Raul's behest. But while Dane had come with Screech to the Reynolds farm, Drake was still apprehensive.

He knew from experience that if Raul and Ken Smith had an interest in you, it meant that you had something that they wanted.

And while Drake still had no idea how Dane fit into this picture, this wasn't a good sign.

He sighed.

At this point, what choice did he have?

Drake leaned over and looked at Screech.

"You still have my brother's number?"

Screech raised an eyebrow, but he eventually pulled out his cell phone and read the number off.

Drake committed it to memory, and then said, "What about you? You want me to take you back to your place?"

Screech shook his head.

"Naw, I think I'll stay here. After all, somebody has to look after the place while you get your beauty sleep," he said, but his voice lacked humor.

"You know, Screech, it's not too late—"

Screech shook his head, effectively cutting Drake off.

"I'm in this," he said calmly. "I'm in this until the end."

It was a strange choice of words—*until the end*—but Drake let it slide.

"I'll just take a nap here," Screech continued. "Then I'll reach out to Yasiv and Dunbar, see if they've got anything on your Russian dude."

Drake nodded.

With that, Screech exited the car and started towards Triple D. He was nearly there when Drake leaned out his window and said, "You're a good friend, Screech. I'm not… I'm not really sure what that means, but I know you're it."

Screech looked like he wanted to say something back, but in the end, he just nodded and walked into Triple D.

***

Drake decided that for the time being the best way to avoid being arrested was to just drive. And as he did, he dialed his brother's number.

He hadn't expected the man to answer and wasn't surprised when he didn't. What did surprise Drake, however, was his willingness to talk to the man's answering machine.

"Dane, it's Damien. Look, I know you were out at the farm, that you helped Screech find me. I also know that Ray was your friend. What I don't know, is what happened between you two all those years ago. Regardless, losing him must hurt." His thoughts turned to Clay. "I've lost someone, too. Someone I was close with. And now… shit, and now I've got myself tangled up in a mess that I don't think I can get out of. What I'm trying to say, is that after this is all done, I might be going away for a while. A *long* while. So… I know I'm rambling here, but if you want to talk, if there's anything you need to tell me, now would be the time. I'm here for you. I'm here for you now, but the truth is, I should have been there for you back then. I should have—"

The answering machine beeped, cutting him off.

"Shit," Drake swore, rubbing his eyes. He was about to toss the phone on the passenger seat when it buzzed in his hand. He stared at it, and for a second he thought he saw the number he'd just called—his brother's number—on the display, but when he blinked, it read *Unlisted*.

The last time he'd gotten a call from an unlisted number, it had been to tell him that the Skeleton King was back.

Drake could only imagine what this was about.

He took a deep breath and answered it.

"Drake."

"Drake, it's Sgt. Yasiv—it's Henry. I've got… shit, she's gone, Drake."

Drake sat bolt upright in the car seat.

"Who? Who's gone?"

His first thought was that Yasiv was talking about Jasmine or maybe Suzan, but that didn't make any sense.

"Speak to me, Yasiv. Who's missing?"

He heard the man take a deep breath on the other end of the line.

"Mandy… she was staying at my house. Everything was fine when we went to sleep last night, but when I woke up… I think she might have climbed out of the window, Drake. And now I have no idea where she is."

Drake slammed his fist on the dash.

"You promised me you'd keep her safe, Yasiv!"

"I know, I know, Drake. I'm sorry. I didn't… shit. I didn't think that she would run away."

A horn honked, and Drake realized that he'd drifted into the center of the road. He gave the other driver the finger and righted his car.

"Does anybody at the precinct know about her?"

"No, I didn't tell anyone. Kramer didn't even remember that she was at the hangar. He thinks that you threw something at him, something that knocked him out. We found nothing there, by the way, nothing but the trails of blood. I even had SCUBA comb the shore, but so far, they haven't come up with anything. But Kramer… shit, you've gone from a person of interest to America's Most Wanted. Palmer is gunning for you, Drake, and this time there's nothing I can do to stop him."

Drake ground his teeth in frustration.

He figured this was coming, but he'd hoped for more time. They had to find out where the next shipment was going to be dropped, they *had* to save the new girls before they ended up in a dumpster with their throats slit like Veronica's friend.

And he'd made a promise to Mandy, one that he intended to keep, no matter the cost.

"I'm close here. I'm close to finding out where these girls were headed. I just need more time."

There was a short pause.

"Yasiv? You still there?"

"You need to be careful, Drake. This mess you've gotten yourself into… I think that you're in real danger. It might be in your best interest to just come in. I can… I can keep you safe."

Drake couldn't believe his ears.

"Keep me safe? Keep *me* safe? You couldn't even keep Mandy safe and nobody knows about her. The cops… the Mayor… they're the ones behind this shit. If I came in, I'd be walking right into their arms. That's what they *want* me to do. I just need more time... one more day. I need to—"

Drake was cut off by the sound of a siren. A second later, cherries lit up his rearview.

"Goddammit, Yasiv! They found me!"

Chapter 35

BECKETT, DRENCHED IN SWEAT and Bob's blood, slid in behind the steering wheel.

He knew that he should get out of there, that he should flee the scene as quickly as possible. But he didn't.

First, he had to be smart; *smarter* than he had been.

Beckett put the syringe and scalpel back in the leather case and tossed it on the passenger seat. The second thing he did was slam his hands against the steering wheel five or six times in rapid succession until his palms started to ache.

"Fuck!" he screamed.

His plan had been terrible, the execution worse, and he'd almost died.

And there was a fucking kid there, an innocent kid who was now scarred for life. All because he'd rushed it. Beckett had been so eager for his next kill, that he'd just run head first into this mess, guns blazing.

This fact bothered him more than nearly being killed by the white hulk; it wasn't at all like him. He was analytical, calculated. But this… this was something else.

This was bloodlust, plain and simple.

And it scared him. It scared him *badly.*

With gritted teeth, Beckett put the car into drive. His only saving grace, he knew, was that he'd been in the fortified room when Bob had attacked him. If it had happened in the kitchen, somebody would have heard them, someone other than a four-year-old boy. If that had been the case, he wouldn't be surprised if the cops were already at his house, waiting for him with a set of handcuffs at the ready.

As the adrenaline finally fled him, Beckett did a quick assessment of his wounds. His ankle was severely twisted and he had a deep bone bruise on his hip. His throat was raw and scratchy and it was still difficult to breathe, but by some miracle, Bob hadn't crushed his hyoid bone.

He'd gotten away lucky.

Or had he.

As Beckett drove slowly down the Manhattan streets in the early dawn, he did a mental inventory of his equipment. The outer glove on his left hand had torn, but the one beneath was still intact. The gloves on his right hand were unblemished.

As far as he could tell, he wasn't bleeding, either, which meant no DNA at the scene.

It was possible that—

"Oh, no," he moaned.

The balaclava!

Beckett whipped his head around to the backseat, then glanced at the floor.

It wasn't there.

He remembered Bob ripping it off, but he couldn't recall grabbing it before getting the hell out of there.

He still had the yacht manifest, but he didn't have his goddamn balaclava. And the way it had been so violently torn from his head… it most definitely had his DNA in it.

Beckett gripped the steering wheel so tightly that his knuckles nearly dislocated. And then he screamed as loud and as hard as he could.

"You fucked up, Beckett! You fucked up real bad this time!"

This wasn't like Craig Sloan or Donnie DiMarco or even Ray Reynolds. Bob Bumacher was a man who had a presence in New York, the same goddamn city that Beckett worked and lived in.

And he'd left his DNA at the scene; his DNA *and* an eyewitness.

Beckett took three deep breaths in through his nose and out through his mouth, trying to calm himself.

It worked… *almost*. He was still furious, but he could sense these feelings taking up residence in his hippocampus so that his cerebrum could focus on the problem at hand.

"Think, Beckett," he said to himself as he pulled into his driveway. "Think about how you can fix this. That's what you do; you're a pathologist. You piece together the evidence, the time of death, the nature of the victim's injuries. Use your goddamn brain, Beckett."

He knew that he had to somehow get the evidence back from the scene, but the first thing he had to do was get rid of the evidence on his person.

Mainly, Bob's blood.

After glancing around to make sure that there were no dog walkers or joggers in the street, Beckett scooped up all his tools and quickly headed up the stairs to his house. He looked around once more as he unlocked the door and, confident that no one had seen him, he slipped inside.

Beckett went directly to the kitchen and pulled out a garbage bag from beneath the sink. Then he made his way upstairs and stepped into the shower still fully clothed. Once inside, he stripped off his gloves and his bloody clothing. He tossed everything, including the small leather case containing the syringe and scalpel, in the garbage bag and did it up tight.

Only then did he turn on the water—scalding – and stood beneath the showerhead. Before long, the water that ran off him went from red to pink to clear. He scrubbed every part of his body from his fingernails to his toenails to make sure that none of Bob's DNA—a single epithelial, a drop of blood, saliva, a tear, anything—remained on his person.

When he was done, he repeated everything from the beginning, starting from the top of his head and working his way down to his toes. Fifteen minutes later, Beckett stepped out of the shower.

During his shower, Beckett's mind had been working in overdrive, trying to figure out a way to get his balaclava back.

He took a seat on the corner of his bed and retrieved another case from the bedside table. Only this one didn't contain a scalpel and syringe; this one contained an amateur tattoo kit.

As he continued to work out a solution to his problem, Beckett lifted his right arm and began the process of inking another tattoo beneath the others. As he worked, he kept repeating the same four names in a whisper.

"Craig Sloan, Donnie DiMarco, Ray Reynolds, Bob Bumacher. Craig Sloan, Donnie DiMarco, Ray Reynolds, Bob Bumacher. Craig Sloan…"

Chapter 36

During his entire career as an NYPD police officer and then as a detective, Damien Drake had been in a grand total of three police chases. And for two of them, he had been relegated to the back of the pack.

But this… this was new for him. This time, *he* was the one being chased by the cops.

Common sense told him to pull over, to try to explain things. But common sense had always been a stranger to Drake. Instead of stopping, he gunned it. Only his car was nearly forty years old and hadn't been in for a tune-up for half that time. To his rusty Crown Vic, flooring it meant a subtle and gradual increase in speed.

"Great," he grumbled. But what his car lacked in speed, Drake made up for in familiarity. He slowed at a stop sign to make it look like he was going to stop, but then made a hard right. The police car followed.

"We're just getting started."

Drake was no longer a police officer, but he knew exactly what techniques they would use, and at what point they were required to just let him go.

The last thing he wanted to do was run someone over, but if he was speeding in a crowded area, the police would eventually back off.

Drake took a left on the next street, as he tried to orient himself in the city. It was coming up on 6:30 AM and New York was starting to come alive. He made another left and spotted a familiar school crossing sign.

He headed straight for it.

The cops must have realized his plan as well, because they tried to pull up beside him. They were going to initiate a precision immobilization technique—the PIT maneuver—in which the front of their car pushed the rear passenger door of Drake's Crown Vic, effectively causing him to spin out of control.

But so long as he drove directly in front of them, this was impossible.

Drake continued to put the pedal to the metal, all the while mumbling at his Crown Vic to get moving.

He was almost at the T-intersection when he saw the school bus. It was traveling perpendicular to him and was starting to chug through the intersection.

Drake grit his teeth and bore down. He had enough faith in both his driving ability and his Crown Vic, but it was still going to be close. Bringing his car all the way to the left side of the road, he got as close to the curb as possible. A split second before he t-boned the bus, he jammed the wheel hard to the left, while at the same time slamming on the brakes.

The Crown Vic was too old to have antilock brakes, which allowed him to skid dramatically through the intersection, passing within inches of the front of the bus.

The driver leaned on the horn, but he ignored the sound. And then, as Drake had predicted, the man braked *hard,* completely blocking the intersection behind him.

Confident that the police car would have to loop back if they were to continue the chase, Drake made several turns down side streets.

After five minutes passed without seeing them again, he felt his body relax.

He'd lost them—for now.

But he knew he wasn't out of the woods yet. His car was too obvious, too conspicuous. As much as the thought pained him, he knew that he had to get rid of it.

Drake drove quickly to the only place that he thought he would be safe, where he could hide out at least until they discovered the location of the auction.

He just hoped that someone was home.

After turning down a narrow alley next to the rundown apartment complex, he got out of his car. The neighborhood was shady, and while he loved his crown Vic dearly, he loved his freedom more.

With a sigh and a gentle caress of the hood, Drake tossed his car keys on the front seat through the half-open window.

"Veronica, you better be home. Because I'm in no shape to do any walking."

Drake knew that within a few hours in this neighborhood, his car would be gone.

Chapter 37

AFTER PUTTING ON A fresh pair of clothes, Beckett took the bag from the shower and threw it in the trunk of his car. As he got behind the wheel, he popped a few caffeine pills that he still had from his late nights in residency and dry swallowed them.

Then he put the car into drive.

Although he had never formally been suspended after what had happened with Craig Sloan, unofficially he had been relegated to paperwork for the time being. And yet, he still had some clout when it came to the junior MEs. If there was a case he wanted, Beckett was fairly certain he could get it.

And there was one in particular that he very much needed to be a part of.

The only problem was, he couldn't rightly request a specific case without raising eyebrows—that wasn't how it worked. And he definitely couldn't request one that hadn't even been called in yet.

Beckett returned to the scene of the crime, cruising slowly around the neighborhood—not so close to Bob's house to raise suspicion, but close enough that he would see the police arrive.

It took nearly an hour before the first squad car appeared.

This was quickly followed by a second and a third.

And yet, Beckett continued to wait. When the air was inundated with both police and ambulance sirens, he started toward the house.

Beckett parked as close to the scene as he could, then hopped out of his car. Almost immediately, a police officer blocked his path.

"I'm sorry, but this street is closed. You're going to have to—"

Beckett pulled out his medical examiner badge and flashed it.

"Dr. Beckett Campbell, ME. I was in the neighborhood and heard the sirens. What's going on?"

The officer hooked a chin toward the door of Bob Bumacher's house.

"It's a fucking shit show in there. It looks like—"

At that moment, a police officer exited the house, his arm draped around the young boy in the pajamas. As the first officer droned on, the boy walked directly in front of Beckett on his way to a squad car.

This was the moment of truth: if the boy saw him, if he recognized Beckett, all bets were off.

The smartest thing to do was to retreat until the boy was gone, but he needed to *know*. He needed to know if the boy remembered him.

Their eyes met and for a split-second recognition seemed to wash over the boy's features. And then, in a blink, it was gone.

Beckett felt the tightness that gripped his organs relax.

The trauma of the incident inside his home had messed with the boy's memories, it seemed. At least for now.

"Yeah?" The officer asked.

Beckett shook his head.

"What's that?"

"I asked if you were on duty, if you're going to come inside. We need a medical examiner to clear the body."

Beckett nodded.

"I've got my bag in the car. You're still going to have to call it in, but when you do, just let him know that Dr. Campbell's already on the scene, that I was in the neighborhood."

The officer agreed and reached for his walkie-talkie to communicate with dispatch.

With a sigh of relief, Beckett walked back to his car and grabbed the bag from the front seat.

One down, one to go, he thought as he made his way toward Bob Bumacher's house.

***

"It looks like the perp gained entry into the home via the window over the sink. Used a crowbar that we found in the safe room."

Beckett raised an eyebrow as he walked from the kitchen to the family room.

"Safe room?"

The officer, a middle-aged man with a paunch around his middle and a thin bristly mustache, shrugged.

"Something like that. The door was reinforced, but the attacker managed to break the lock. We found a couple of shotguns and a bag of heroin inside. I already called in some techs to work on the computer… if I were a betting man, I'd bet the house on finding something naughty on it."

As Beckett strode over to the room, the reek of coagulated blood that hung in the air grew stronger.

The sheer violence of the scene took his breath away. Even though it had been his doing, Beckett could barely wrap his mind around what he saw.

A shirtless Bob Bumacher was lying on his back with his right arm curled beneath him. There was a gaping hole in his neck roughly the size of a softball, and blood pooled beneath his bald head and coated his bare chest.

The officer who squatted by the body looked up as Beckett approached.

"Dr. Campbell, ME."

The officer nodded, then said, "Looks like he bled out."

No shit, Sherlock.

"Also, there's something in his hand," the officer continued, reaching for Bob's right arm. "Looks like—"

"Don't touch the body," Beckett ordered. "No one is to touch the body before I clear it."

The officer recoiled and put his hands in the air.

"Shit, sorry. I wasn't going to touch it, I just wanted to show you something."

Beckett frowned.

"Nobody's to touch the body," he repeated in a condescending tone.

The officer grumbled something about how he hated doctors, but retreated behind Beckett without addressing him directly.

Heart racing, Beckett walked over to Bob and stared down at his body for a moment, trying to act normal.

But there was nothing normal about the situation.

I did this, he thought absently. *I was the one responsible for this carnage.*

Beckett squatted, positioning himself between the body and the door, hoping that he was blocking the police officer's line of sight. Then he set his black bag down on top of Bob's right arm.

After slipping a pair of lab gloves on, he did a routine overview of the body, as he always did. First, he checked for a pulse—there was none, of course—and then set about looking for any wounds on the man's body aside from the obvious. There was only one: a small red pinprick of blood on his left biceps from where the needle of Midazolam had struck him. But Beckett only saw this because he knew what to look for.

It would take at least a few days for anyone else to notice, and a week or so for the tox screen to come back. That would give him enough time to erase any evidence that he'd been here.

Or so Beckett hoped.

Working quickly, he reached into his bag and took out a large plastic specimen container and a pair of tweezers. Then he used the latter to inspect Bob's ruined neck, pretending to search for any fragments of a weapon that might have remained in the wound.

As he performed this charade, Beckett used his other hand to reach into the bag again and grab the clean balaclava from within.

Then, with a sleight-of-hand that would make even the most expert of magicians proud, Beckett placed this new balaclava over the old one. Rigor had already started to set in, and it took a sharp yank to free the balaclava from the man's dead fingers, which Beckett disguised by pretending to momentarily lose his balance. This distraction also allowed him to put the original balaclava into his bag without being seen.

Satisfied, Beckett stood and turned back to the officer whose gaze was transfixed on the corpse.

"Well? Any ideas?" the man asked excitedly.

"Ideas?" Beckett repeated with a frown. "My idea is that the guy is dead. Bag his hands and get CSU in here as soon as possible."

Chapter 38

"DON'T TASE ME," DRAKE said, his arms in the air. "Veronica, it's me. If you're in there, please don't tase me."

A sleepy-looking Veronica opened the door, sans Taser, Drake noted.

"Drake? What are you doing here? I told you—"

"I need a place to crash, Veronica."

Veronica observed him suspiciously for a moment, before stepping aside.

"I may not have my Taser on me, but if you try anything, I won't hesitate to get it out."

Drake shook his head as he stepped inside the apartment.

"I'm not—"

He stopped cold. Mandy was seated at the vanity brushing her long blond hair.

"Mandy? What the hell are you doing here? Sgt. Yasiv said that…" he let his sentence trail off as Mandy turned to look at him.

"I couldn't stay there," she said as if this simple explanation was sufficient.

It wasn't.

"What do you mean, you couldn't stay there?"

Before Mandy could answer, Veronica stepped between them.

"I found her wandering the streets, Drake, near where you dropped me off. As soon as I started talking to her, I realized that this was the girl you and Screech told me about… I took her under my wing, and—"

Drake's eyes bulged.

"You *what*? You took her under your wing? You had her turning—"

Something in Veronica's face changed then. Her pretty features suddenly became ugly and she stepped forward and pinched the back of Drake's arm.

"Come with me," she hissed. "Come with me right now before I tase your ass."

Drake was too exhausted and confused to resist and allowed himself to be guided toward the side of the room opposite Mandy. Veronica pushed aside an ornamental curtain, revealing a doorknob. In a flash, she opened the door and shoved Drake through.

The entire sequence passed as a blur to Drake; he had no idea that there was a separate room adjacent to this one, let alone a full apartment, like the one he found himself in now.

The decor was simple yet classy, but before Drake could take it all in, Veronica pinched his arm again and drew his attention back.

"Don't you do that," she said in a harsh tone. "Don't you fucking do that."

Drake's brow knitted.

"Do what?"

"Don't you judge me—me or her. The girl back there? She's an adult. If she wants to work the streets, she can work the streets. This is my job, Drake, my profession. And I'm good at it—*damn* good at it. I'm not some meth-head who's only turning tricks to get my next high, and neither is she. This is my—*our*—choice, and you have no right to judge us."

Drake was taken aback by the woman's outburst.

In truth, he hadn't really put much into what Veronica did. He knew from his past experience with Veronica that she dealt with affluent clients who paid big money to spend the night with her. And she could most definitely take care of herself. And yet, when the woman had mentioned that she'd taken Mandy under her wing, something just felt intrinsically wrong.

But it wasn't *wrong*. Sure, it might be illegal, but that was bullshit—an archaic law based on some religious nonsense that no longer held any meaning. Who was he to tell a woman what she could or couldn't do with her own body? Provided that it was safe and voluntary, what right did *anyone* have to tell a woman how they plied their trade, be it basket weaving or prostitution?

Drake lowered his eyes, suddenly feeling ashamed.

"I'm sorry, it's just that she was exploited back and—"

Veronica pinched him again.

"I'm not exploited and I don't exploit people. I resent the accusation."

Drake apologized a second time.

"I didn't mean it that way—look, Veronica, I'm sorry. I'm exhausted and I just need a place to crash."

Veronica looked him up and down, and it soon became clear that it was her who felt sorry for him and not the other way around.

"If anybody's being exploited here, it's you," she said with conviction.

Me? Exploited? By whom?

But Drake couldn't mount these questions; he could barely think straight.

"This way," she said and Drake followed.

Veronica led him to a bedroom that couldn't be more opposite to the one he'd just exited. Whereas he was used to the massive bedposts and dozens of various sized pillows in the main room, this one contained only a simple, plain wooden bed.

"Lie down, get some rest. When you wake up, I'll tell you what I found out about the auction."

Drake was in the process of doing just that—lying down—when Veronica mentioned the auction. He tried to sit back up, to ask questions, but he'd reached the point of no return.

He was out in seconds.

Chapter 39

NORMALLY AFTER VISITING A crime scene, Beckett returned to the hospital to fill out forms. Only this time, after jotting a few notes—mostly for show given that he knew the exact time and cause of death—he went back to his apartment. There, he showered again as a final precaution: if the crime was ever linked back to him, the police would tear his place apart looking for evidence. They would scour the sinks, the drain, the damn sewer pipe if they had to. If they found something from Bob in his house, he'd now have a logical explanation for it being there, given that he was the lead ME on the case.

Finally satisfied, Beckett inspected the tattoo that he'd given himself, made sure that there were no signs of infection, and rubbed some antibiotic ointment on it. Then he got dressed again in something new. The caffeine pills he'd taken earlier had started to wear off, so Beckett brewed himself a nice, strong pot of coffee.

Sipping his coffee, Beckett pulled the yacht manifest out of his pocket. It detailed plans to leave from Manhattan Harbor at 9 AM, and arrive in Colombia four days later. It even had the projected ocean currents and weather all mapped out.

Four days to get to Colombia, one day to pick up the cargo, four days to get back, Beckett thought, *with a stop in the Virgin Gorda on the return leg.*

This was something he couldn't let happen. Even if the girls managed to survive the journey this time, if the heroin laced with fentanyl derivatives made it onto US soil, the number of overdoses would be astronomical.

He tapped the side of his coffee mug.

Despite having the manifest in his hand, hard evidence that Bob was involved in this scheme, something still wasn't adding up: the girls were found in a shipping container, not on a yacht.

Beckett closed his eyes and thought back to his time in the Virgin Gorda when he'd first seen *B-Yacht'ch.*

There were the models, the ones that Donnie DiMarco was taking photos of, and there was the skid of heroin. There definitely weren't any shipping containers, though, at least none that he could recall. But Beckett didn't completely trust his memory; after all, he'd been drunk half the time and high the rest.

Could I have missed the shipping containers? Or was I just plain wrong about Bob? Was it all just a fucked up coincidence that the man had stolen a yacht that transported the girls? Maybe the manifest was something he just found on board. Maybe… maybe Bob wasn't part of this at all.

An image of Bob's mangled neck flashed in Beckett's mind and he swallowed hard.

No, Bob was behind this… wasn't he?

He pulled his cell phone out of his pocket and scrolled through his contacts. The phone rang four times before a groggy voice answered.

"Hello?"

"Screech, it's your vacay pal, Beckett."

"Yeah? What's up?"

"Let me ask you something… do you remember any container ships in the Virgin Gorda? Docked at the place we were staying?"

There was a short pause.

"No—there couldn't be. Those things are massive, they can't just pull up to a regular dock. It would be like parking an eighteen-wheeler in a cigarette ashtray."

Beckett's heart sunk.

"But… remember when Bob took us to St. Thomas?" Screech continued. "The mainland? We passed a tanker that was about a half-hour offshore."

Bingo, Beckett thought. *That's where they transferred the girls to the containers—offshore. Makes sense; then it would be one of hundreds or even thousands of containers, and much more difficult to find than if the girls were just on the yacht.*

How it got to the shore afterward was another issue altogether, but Beckett had the information he needed.

And peace of mind; Bob *was* involved.

"Why do you ask?"

"I'm just trying to work out the logistics of how the girls made it from Colombia to New York," Beckett said, staring down at the manifest. "Listen, last time we spoke, you mentioned something about a Russian guy?"

"His name is Boris… Boris Brackovich. Looks to be involved in high-end commercial real estate, but that's all I've got for now. I sent his name over to Yasiv and Dunbar to see what they can dig up, but I haven't heard anything yet."

Beckett's eyes narrowed at the mention of the police officers, but before he could say anything, Screech continued.

"But Drake… Drake found something. Something about the girls, how they weren't just recruited to be prostitutes, but that they were going to be sold in an auction. And the girl who survived the journey? Mandy? She was with Drake, but he passed her off on Yasiv. But now he called and said she's missing, that she just up and took off in the middle of the night. No one knows where she went."

Beckett tried to soak all this in, but Screech was speaking far too quickly for him to grasp everything.

Mandy's gone?

"Slow down, Screech. Did Mandy run off or did someone—this Boris guy—grab her to tie up loose ends? And what are you talking about, an auction?"

Screech broke it all down for him in a minute and a half. When the man was done, Beckett exhaled loudly. Then he pictured the surprise on Bob's face when he jammed the scalpel repeatedly into his neck and throat.

Yeah, Beckett thought with a modicum of satisfaction. *Bob was a bad dude. A bad dude who got what he deserved.*

"And you guys are sure that they're going to go ahead with another auction? Any idea when and where it's going to take place?"

"We're pretty sure, yeah. Got a tip from someone who works the streets. But as for when or where, I—*we*—have no idea."

Beckett chewed the inside of his lip. It was clear to him now that even though he was confident that Bob was involved, he was low down the food chain. After all, they'd spent time together on the yacht and while Bob wasn't stupid, he wouldn't have the connections or the foresight to put together an auction.

Auction... selling girls as sex slaves.

The thought was enough to send a shiver up his spine.

Beckett checked his watch. It was nearly 8 o'clock; if he hurried, he could incinerate his bloody clothes and the balaclava back at the lab, file his preliminary report on Bob Bumacher, and still make it to the yacht before it set off.

He had a feeling that the yacht would leave with or without the white hulk, and whoever was on that boat would be one step higher than Bob Bumacher.

"All right, I'll see what I can do for my end," he said.

"What you mean?" Screech asked, suddenly sounding accusatory.

"Nothing. Just that if I hear or see anything in the morgue, I'll let you know. And if anything comes up on your end, don't be a stranger."

Another pause.

"Okay," Screech replied hesitantly. "Everything alright with you, Beckett?"

A series of names flashed in Beckett's mind.

Craig Sloan… Donnie DiMarco… Ray Reynolds… Bob Bumacher…

"I'm fine. I just want to catch these bastards."

"Yeah, if we can find them."

Beckett focused on the yacht manifest in his hand.

Unlike Screech, he wasn't worried about finding the men responsible, he was more concerned with what he would do to them once he did.

Chapter 40

DRAKE AWOKE WITH A start. At first, he didn't know where he was, which was becoming an all too common occurrence for his liking. But as his vision began to clear, he realized that he was in Veronica's second bedroom. He sat up and was startled to find Veronica sitting in a chair across the room, staring at him.

"Wow, that's creepy," he said, clearing his throat.

Veronica smiled and held a half-full glass out to him.

Drake eyed the substance curiously. It was slightly viscous and had a mild yellow tinge to it.

"Water?"

Veronica shook her head.

"Vodka. Sorry, but I'm fresh out of Scotch."

When Drake tried to bring the glass to his lips, he realized that his hand was trembling. He swallowed a mouthful.

"Was I shaking in my sleep?"

Veronica nodded.

"Like a squirrel with Parkinson's."

Drake took another big swig of Vodka. As he did, he recalled the last thing Veronica had said before he'd fallen asleep.

"What about the auction?" he asked. "Did you find something out?"

Any humor that had been in Veronica's pretty face vanished.

"Yeah, you should get dressed. We've only got a few hours."

Drake felt the muscles in his abdomen tighten and his liver burped.

"A few hours? What—"

"It's almost seven o'clock, Drake. The auction starts at nine."

Drake turned his head to face the window, and even though the sheer curtains were closed, he could see that it was already starting to get dark.

Seven o'clock? In the evening? *Holy shit,* Drake thought, *I must've slept for nearly twelve hours.*

He rubbed his eyes.

"Veronica, what are you talking about? What the hell is going on?"

Veronica shook her head.

"Get dressed, Drake. And then we'll talk."

Drake looked down at himself and was surprised to see that he was only wearing his boxers.

What the fuck is going on?

He was confident that he had gone to bed fully clothed. In fact, he remembered just collapsing on the bed and passing out.

Drake turned his eyes back to Veronica.

"Why am I half naked? Did we..."

Veronica rose from the chair and started for the door.

"You wish, Drake. You wish."

***

"They're desperate," Veronica said as the three of them, herself, Drake, and Mandy, sat at the kitchen table. Drake had switched out his vodka for a cup of coffee, while Mandy and Veronica sipped glasses of ice water. "I was on the street for less than an hour last night before I was approached by a man asking us if we wanted to be 'safe'—the same thing that they told Nancy a couple of years back. He handed me the business card you see there on the table."

Drake's eyes drifted down to the black and pink card on the table. In the center was the picture of the legs. The only other thing on the card was a telephone number.

"I wouldn't bother trying to trace the number or anything like that. I can guarantee that it just connects to a burner phone. Speaking of which," Veronica slid Drake's cell phone over to him and he picked it up. When it wouldn't turn on, he raised an eyebrow. Veronica handed over the battery next. "We took the battery out; I'm pretty sure as soon as you plug it back in, the cops are going to be all over it."

Drake picked up both parts of the phone, debated putting it together, but then changed his mind and placed them back down.

Veronica was right. DI Palmer would do anything and everything to bring him in. Tracing his phone would be a given.

"So, are you gonna call these guys?" he asked.

Veronica glanced at Mandy and then both of them shook their heads. There was something in that exchange that tipped Drake off and his eyes narrowed.

"Not happening," he said. "There's no way in hell I'm going to let you do this."

As before when Veronica had dragged him into the adjacent apartment, her expression turned ugly.

Drake decided to take a different approach.

"This isn't your fight, Veronica. It's going to be dangerous and you yourself said that we shouldn't get involved with these guys. Leave it to the pros."

Even as the words came out of his mouth, Drake cringed, expecting the backlash that was coming.

"*Pros*?" Veronica repeated with a hint of a smile. "Pros like you? Like you, who was banging on my door at six-thirty in the morning begging to be let in? Rambling about needing to get away from the cops? Those kinds of pros?"

Drake sighed.

"Look, I'm just—"

Veronica rolled her eyes.

"You just what, dad? Want me to get a real job? Go to college, maybe? Rack up $120,000 worth of debt only to work at McDonald's and spend the rest of my life paying it off to some rich assholes? No thanks, Drake."

"I'm—"

"I don't care what you do, Drake. But I *know* what I'm doing," Veronica interrupted again.

It was next to impossible to get a word in edgewise with this woman.

"When you first got here and asked about the auction, you're right: I had no interest in getting involved. But now that I know Mandy and I know what happened to her friends? Her family? I'm going to do whatever I can to help stop this, like I should have done when Nancy ended up in the dumpster. You want to know why? I'll tell you why: because these aren't just people. These are *my* people. And I *will* go to that auction tonight, and so will Mandy. If you try to stop me..." Veronica let her sentence trail off as she pulled the Taser from behind her back and crackled the leads.

Drake sighed again, feeling the weight of the world slide off his shoulders, only to be repositioned on top of his head. There was no way to talk Veronica out of this. Absolutely no way.

The only thing he could do was come up with a plan that would keep them all safe, keep them alive for at least one more night.

And for once, Drake thought that he might be able to do just that.

"Let me use your phone," he said. Veronica hesitated, but eventually handed it over. "I've got an idea."

Without looking at her, he dialed a number. A man answered on the first ring.

"Screech, I need your help. I need your computer skills."

"I'm listening," his partner said.

After outlining his plan to Screech, Drake hung up and immediately dialed another number.

"Yasiv, it's Drake. I know you're probably losing your shit right now, but I think I found a way out of this for you, for me, for everyone. You just be ready..."

And then Drake relayed the plan to the sergeant of 62nd precinct.

"You do know what this means, don't you?" the man asked when he was done. "For you, I mean."

Drake nodded and pinched the bridge of his nose. He was well aware of the consequences of his plan.

"Yeah, I know. Just be ready."

Drake hung up the phone and slid it across the table to a wide-eyed Veronica.

"Does that work for you guys?"

Mandy and Veronica exchanged a look and then turned back to him. They nodded in unison.

"Now what? What do we do for the next two hours?" Veronica asked.

Drake shrugged.

"Well, for one, you can start with getting me more vodka."

PART III

Everything has its Price

Chapter 41

VERONICA WIPED THE LIPSTICK from the corners of her mouth and smoothed the front of her skirt. Then she looked over at Mandy, who was staring down the street, a far-off look in her eyes.

"You okay?" she asked.

Mandy turned to face her.

"I'm fine. I just… I just wanted to thank you for what you're doing for me. For my friends."

Veronica shrugged.

"I'm doing it for us, honey. I'm doing it so that no one else has to die in a shipping container or get tossed into a dumpster like a piece of trash. The fact that we work in the sex trade has no bearing on our worth or value as human beings."

"I knew what we were getting into was dangerous," Mandy started, eyes downcast. "We all did. But we never—"

"Listen to me: charging money for sex is a transaction, that's it. It doesn't—"

A gray cube van suddenly approached and Veronica went silent. It pulled up next to them and the window slowly rolled down. A man with a shaved head and gold incisor peered out.

It was the same man who had approached them yesterday. Veronica put on her best fake smile and looked over at Mandy. She was surprised to see that the girl was doing the same. She might be young, but she definitely wasn't inexperienced. And Veronica got the distinct impression that her timid exterior was just a front. In truth, Mandy appeared anything *but* scared, which was disconcerting to Veronica.

Because she was downright terrified.

"You girls looking for a good time?" the man with the Russian accent said with a chuckle. "Just kidding. Get in the back of the van."

Veronica's eyes narrowed and she pulled her purse, which contained the Taser, closer to her body.

"I thought you said—"

"Yes, yes, yes. But my client… he is very, well, how can I say this… he is very rich. You need to get in the van, because you can't know where he lives. Trust me, it's safe."

I wouldn't trust you with my pet gerbil, Veronica thought. *I'd be gone for less than ten minutes before you had it halfway up your ass.*

"Okay, but I've got people looking out for me," Veronica said. "If I'm not back in a few hours, they'll come looking."

The man's smile grew.

"I'm sure you do, sweetheart. Just get in the van before I change my mind," he looked at Mandy and gave her a wink. "You too, beautiful."

When Drake had first come up with this plan, Veronica had been concerned that one of the men involved in the auction might recognize Mandy. But now, seeing the way that the Russian man in the truck leered at her, it was clear that this wasn't the case. Mandy wasn't a person to them, she was a thing. A thing that they could play with, something with which to exercise their darkest, most sadistic fantasies. And when they were done with her? Out with the trash, and in with the new.

"Okay," Veronica said hesitantly. She looked at Mandy and then together they walked around the back of the van. As they approached, the doors swung open and two men stared at them. Unlike the driver, these men weren't smiling. The one on the left held out a thick hand covered in wiry black hair.

"Purse," he said in an accent so thick that it was almost impossible to understand.

"Excuse me?" Veronica asked.

The man wiggled his sausage-like fingers.

"Purse," he repeated.

When Veronica didn't immediately hand it over, the other man stepped forward. Although he wasn't smiling either, his demeanor was less harsh than sausage fingers.

"It's just for safety. We can't have you taking selfies with the client. He is a very rich and powerful man. Once you're done, you'll get it back. I promise."

Veronica clutched the bag to her chest.

She was playing a game, acting a role so as to not raise suspicion, but couldn't imagine how anybody with any degree of common sense would enter the van with these two bozos.

"Either you give me your purse or you go home. You can't get in with your purse."

Veronica reluctantly handed it over.

"Okay, but I know exactly what's in there, and everything better be still there when I get it back," she said.

Her feigned naïveté was so saccharine that it was making her sick to her stomach.

The man took the purse and nodded.

"I promise," he said again, reaching out and helping Veronica into the van. Sausage fingers did the same for Mandy.

It reeked of stale cigarettes and sweat.

"Where are we—" but before Veronica could finish her sentence, the van doors slammed closed. And then it took off, accelerating so quickly that she fell on her ass. "Hey, what the fuck! What are you—"

But this time her sentence was cut off by a fabric hood that was pulled over her head.

Veronica tried to struggle, but before she knew what was happening, her hands were bound behind her back.

"It's for your own protection," one of the Russians said. "Don't worry, it'll all be over soon."

Veronica couldn't be sure, but she thought she also heard him laugh.

Chapter 42

DRAKE WATCHED ANXIOUSLY AS the van pulled up next to the two girls and a man started chatting with them. He was too far away to hear exactly what was being said, but judging by Veronica's reactions, this was the encounter that they'd expected.

The woman knew that things were likely to get a little rough, and she'd been willing to take that risk.

But when both girls were hoisted up into the back of the van by two gruff-looking men, Drake couldn't help but grind his teeth. Sitting in Veronica's Tesla across the street with the lights off, he felt helpless. No, he felt more than helpless. He felt like a fucking invalid.

The plan that he'd concocted was relatively simple, but the thing that worried him the most was the sheer number of people involved. Too many people had a role to play and even if one of them missed their mark, no matter how minor, bad things could happen. Like the bad thing that had happened to the young street worker that had been found in the dumpster. That kind of bad.

Right now, Ken Smith and ANGUIS Holdings had all the leverage. They had photographs of him, of Beckett, and worst of all of Jasmine. All Drake had were some transient links between the Mayor and a clandestine holdings company. Drake was positive that it was all connected to the Church of Liberation and Ken Smith's time in Colombia. He was also fairly certain that Ken wasn't just using the church to use Ray Reynolds's and his men to take out anyone who might oppose them, but to also wash money from illegal operations.

But he had no real proof of any of this. Drake had spent enough time in front of lawyers to know that even public defenders would chew holes through his theories like pastrami on rye. It didn't make it any less true, of course, but if a public defender could do that, he couldn't imagine what the head of one of the largest and most prestigious law firms in all of New York City would be able to come up with. No, they needed real tangible, *irrefutable* proof.

And the only way to get it, so far as Drake could see, was by putting themselves in dangerous situations. Drake only wished that it was him risking everything, and not Veronica and Mandy.

The van pulled away, and Drake, eyes narrowed, put the Tesla into drive and followed.

Chapter 43

BECKETT ONLY GOT PART of what he wanted accomplished. He managed to file his preliminary report on Bob Bumacher, but the traffic was so bad in Manhattan that the drive took twice as long as he'd anticipated. As a result, he wasn't able to toss his bloody clothes in the incinerator. It made him nervous to keep them with him a second longer than he had to, but they were better off in the trunk of his car than taking the risk of getting caught with them half-baked in the oven.

In the end, with some aggressive driving and a lucky streak of green lights, Beckett made it to the port with ten minutes to spare.

He parked across from the main parking lot in a spot that offered him a clear view of the ostentatious yacht. Judging by the way the electronic devices on the roof whirred and spun, it was clear that it was preparing to depart.

And yet, Beckett was in no hurry to get out of his car. The colossal fuck up at Bob Bumacher's house was still fresh in his mind, as was the face of the poor kid who had walked in on them. He assumed that based on the fact the media wasn't all over this already, that they found something incriminating on Bob's computer to go with the heroin he'd planted. And if that were the case, he'd gone from a poor workingman slain in front of his son, to a criminal mastermind who had been taken out by his competition, and they were scrambling to change their scripts.

He glanced over at the leather case on the passenger seat that had been loaded with not one but three syringes of Midazolam, two scalpels, and a pair of surgical shears.

That's your idea of being prepared? Not scoping out the place, planning and expertly carrying out a silent attack, but just bringing more weapons?

Beckett sighed and rubbed his eyes. He was exhausted and his body was riddled with bruises and pain from his encounter with Bob. And yet he didn't have time to sleep.

He scooped up the case from the passenger seat and slid it into the pocket of his shorts. Then he looked up at himself in the mirror.

"What are you doing, Beckett?" he asked himself.

It was a rhetorical question, of course, and yet he still felt the need to answer.

You're making those assholes pay. You're making these assholes pay for murdering your student Dr. Eddie Larringer, for almost killing Suzan Cuthbert, for convincing a group of depressed ex-criminals to poison themselves, for being responsible for the overdose of more than two dozen girls in a shipping container. That's *what you're doing.*

You're making them pay.

You're going to make them all *pay.*

Chapter 44

ABOUT HALFWAY THROUGH THEIR trip to wherever the Russians were taking them, Veronica started to think that this whole thing was a bad idea.

A *very* bad idea.

It wasn't just the hood over her face or her bound hands, although this was more than she expected, it was the silence. She could hear the men breathing and the occasional flick of a lighter as one of them lit a cigarette. But other than that, they didn't speak. They didn't speak to her or to Mandy or to each other. And this was disconcerting, to say the least.

It was as if everyone in the van knew that the girls were being driven to their death.

In her mind, Veronica tried to concentrate on the route that they were taking, using an old trick she'd come up with as a kid. She'd sit with her eyes closed in the backseat of her father's Lexus and count the number of seconds that passed before each turn, note the direction, and divide that by the average driving speed. When they got home, her dad would get her to draw the route that she thought they'd taken on a map.

More often than not, Veronica got it close to exact. In this case, however, the van kept accelerating and making so many sharp turns that she quickly lost track of any direction at all.

Which was clearly the point.

The passage of time was also hard to determine, given that her senses were occluded by the hood over her head. If she had to guess, she would've pegged the entire trip to have taken anywhere between thirty minutes to an hour, although she wouldn't have been at all surprised if Drake told her later that it was closer to two hours.

If he could keep up with them, that is.

Eventually, the van started to reverse and then came to an abrupt stop. A moment later, she was gruffly hoisted to her feet.

"Can you loosen my hands?" Veronica asked. Her words were muffled by the hood, but she was certain that they could understand her; they just chose not to answer. She was lowered out of the back of the van, and heard Mandy struggling beside her. "Just relax, Mandy. They're going to take care of us."

As if to reinforce this point, someone hooked an arm in hers, and Veronica was led slowly away from the van. She walked for about twenty paces before she was handed off to someone else. A door was opened, words were exchanged in Russian, and then Veronica felt the temperature and texture of the air change as she was forced inside.

"Can you—"

Veronica was going to ask to have her bindings loosened again when her hands were suddenly, and thankfully, cut free. At the same time, her hood was pulled from behind and removed.

The next series of events were as confusing as they were frightening.

The room that Veronica found herself in was nearly pitch black, but she could see just enough to know that Mandy was beside her. There was someone else behind her as well, but she only knew this because they were in the process of cutting off her dress. Before she could even protest, her dress was gone, leaving her wearing only her thong. But a second later, that too was sliced and pulled away like an expert surgeon severing an artery.

"Hey!" she shouted and whipped around. Veronica just caught sight of a man as he retreated out of a seamless door behind her. "You should've just asked me to take it off! That shit's expensive! Now what am I going to wear home?"

Veronica glanced over at Mandy, and she saw that the girl was also nude. She also looked frightened for the first time since they'd met.

"Did you hear me?" Veronica shouted as she glanced around to try and catch her bearings.

They were standing in a room about the size of a large shower stall, surrounded by what appeared to be glass walls. But they weren't normal glass; they were blacked out, making it impossible for Veronica to see through them. The only illumination came from a dim red bulb maybe twelve feet overhead. Veronica found that if she concentrated on the area that she'd seen the man with the shears leave, she could make out a thin line forming the perimeter of a door, but there was no handle or lock to speak of.

Veronica reached out and pounded on the glass with her palms, more to get a feel of its strength rather than an attempt to break through it.

"Hey! Hey anyone out there!"

The walls felt like Plexiglass; they had a slight give to them, which suggested that there was open air behind it.

And most likely people watching me right now, she thought.

"This is fucked up! I didn't—"

There was a loud buzz and then the red light above them blinked out. Once they were bathed in darkness, Veronica heard another click, and then Mandy shouted. Veronica reached for her friend, but only managed to graze her leg, which was kicking furiously, before she felt the air pressure change again, followed by another click.

When the red light came on a second later, Veronica found herself alone.

"Hey! Let me out of here!" she shouted. "Let me the fuck out of here!"

This time when Veronica pounded on the Plexiglas walls, she was trying to smash her way through.

Chapter 45

BECKETT WALKED BRISKLY DOWN the dock, keeping his head low and avoiding eye contact with several other patrons who were busy fiddling with their sailboats or tinkering with outboard motors.

Because of the size of the yacht, it had to be moored on a separate extension that stretched out into water deep enough to contain it. This posed a problem for Beckett, as it was the only boat on the extension, which was also roped off; short of getting in the water himself, something he loathed to do, he didn't see how he would be able to sneak up on its occupants.

But as he walked closer, he saw a small leisure craft tied up just before the extension. It had a small 9.9 horsepower motor, the kind that looked like a modified lawn mower, and it appeared as if either the person had forgotten to remove the gas tank, or he was planning to take off shortly.

Without thinking, Beckett strode up to the boat and stepped inside. It rocked, but he somehow avoided tipping it.

Fucking hell… people actually go out to sea in a thing like this?

He sat on the metal seat and stared at the yacht, trying to figure out how many people were onboard. He knew little of boats, and less of yachts, but from his experience on B-Yacht'ch, he knew that it required a crew of at least a half-dozen people to drive the damn thing. And that didn't take into account Bob's smuggling buddies.

Before he could see anybody onboard, however, he heard two people approaching. Beckett quickly turned and buried his head, pretending to be working on the antique motor.

In his periphery, he caught sight of two men walking past.

"No sign of Bob? No one's even heard from him?"

"Maybe he got cold feet. You saw how pissed he was when he found out what happened to the girls."

"We'll wait five more minutes, but then we're taking off, with or without him."

When they were by the pleasure craft, Beckett turned his head and caught a glimpse of the man closest to him.

The man was wearing a pair of pale blue khakis and a white button-down shirt. He had slicked black hair and was cleanly shaven. With his straight nose and dark eyes, he was handsome and also unmistakably recognizable.

It was the mayor's son. Beckett had seen the man on TV several times, Wesley or Watney or Weasel, first when his brother Thomas had been killed and again when Ken Smith was campaigning for mayor.

"No way," he muttered under his breath. Drake was going to like this. Drake was going to like this *a lot*.

The other man was bigger than the mayor's son, with a square frame and muscular shoulders. But because he was on the other side of Wesley Smith, Beckett couldn't get a good look at him.

Beckett stopped tinkering with the motor and pulled the satchel out of his pocket.

I don't need to take out anybody on the boat. I can just hit them here, slide their bodies into the water, and get back to my car without anyone seeing.

Both men were wearing shorts, and he knew that he could slice one, or both, of their femoral arteries before they knew what had happened.

He didn't like the idea of doing this out in the open, but it was better than on a boat with god only knows how many other witnesses. A quick glance around revealed that the dozen or so people on the dock were utterly transfixed in their own worlds.

It's now or never... if they leave, more girls are going to die.

Beckett felt the familiar tingle in his fingertips that he'd experienced on the other four occasions he'd killed.

It was now... it had to be now.

Beckett somehow managed to get out of the boat without rocking it, while at the same time pulling a scalpel from his bag. It was as if time itself had slowed down, as if he was walking through a lucid dream.

Like he was in control of everything.

He closed the distance between them to ten feet, then five. Wesley unhooked the rope to the private dock extension and as he did, the second man turned his head ever so slightly.

It took all of Beckett's willpower not to moan the word *no*.

Even though he'd only caught a glimpse of the man's profile, there was no mistaking who he was, either.

The first and only time that Beckett had seen this man, he'd been half out of his mind on sleeping pills and half dead from methadone poisoning.

But even if he'd never seen the man before in his life, Beckett would've recognized him.

He would've recognized him because he looked exactly like his friend Drake.

But it wasn't Drake; it was his brother.

Breathing heavily, Beckett managed to spin around, even though he'd lost all feeling in his limbs. And then he stumbled all the way back to his car and collapsed behind the wheel.

"Fuck!" he screamed once inside. "Fuck! Fuck! *Fuck!*"

Chapter 46

SCREECH SMILED AS HE cranked away at his keyboard. Because of the backdoor rootkit that he'd installed on Ken's computer, it was a breeze hacking into it and completing his role in Drake's plan.

"*Aaaaand* done," he said.

He leaned back in his chair and interlaced his fingers behind his head, a proud smile on his face.

His pleasure was short-lived.

Mandy's face flashed in his mind, not the way she'd looked when she had stepped into his living room completely nude, but when she'd first knocked on the door of Triple D.

Screech saw the greasy hair hanging in front of her face, her tear-filled eyes.

"Shit," he muttered.

Just as he was going to call Drake and let him know that his part was done, an email notification popped up.

Even though Screech didn't recognize the sender, the headline caught his attention: *Russia.*

Screech opened the email and scanned the contents. The main body was dominated by some sort of rap sheet from Russia. In the upper left-hand corner, there was a picture of Boris Brackovich, as well as his name.

The rest was in Russian, but thankfully the sender had made annotations in the margin. They were just point form notes, but they were more than enough.

It appeared as if Boris had been arrested twice for running a prostitution ring in Chechnya. Further down, there was an accusation of murder against his first wife, a woman named Ivanka Brackovich.

Screech whistled.

Beneath the scanned, annotated image were several lines of typed text.

Had to dig deep to get this—every other record seems to have disappeared. None of the charges stuck. My contact informed me that Boris is wanted for questioning in the deaths of three prostitutes, but he moved to New York eleven years ago before they could get to him.

Hope this helps, D.

PS. If you see Drake, tell him he needs to lay low. He needs to get out of the city and stay out.

"Thanks, Dunbar," Screech whispered.

He stared at Boris's face, a scowl on his own.

You killed those girls, you sick fuck. You killed Mandy's friends.

There was no question in his mind that this man was the one behind the sick auction. The only problem was, Screech had no idea what to do with this information.

Going to the police with it made no sense given that they were likely involved and it had come from them in the first place. And while his first instinct was to reach out to Drake, he decided against it. The man had enough on his plate, enough problems and issues to deal with.

Screech buried his head in his hands and breathed deeply.

He saw Mandy's face again.

There was only one person he could call, one person who could make a difference. And even though every strand of his moral fiber told him not to do it, something had to be done about this sick bastard.

Screech picked up his phone and quickly dialed a number before he changed his mind.

On the second ring, a hoarse voice answered.

"Beckett? It's Screech. I've got… I've got something for you."

Chapter 47

THE GRAY VAN TWISTED and turned through Manhattan, clearly trying to lose any tails that the girls might've had. If he'd been in his Crown Vic, Drake was certain he would have lost them. But his Crown Vic was long gone and Veronica's Tesla was an engineering marvel.

Drake eventually caught up to them in Hell's Kitchen when they backed down an alley between a Chinese restaurant and a massage parlor. This proved problematic; the alley was only slightly wider than the van itself, making it next to impossible to see down the side, let alone squeeze down.

He parked across the street and hurried into the Chinese restaurant. He took a seat at a table near the windows, which were conveniently aimed toward the alley. From this vantage point, he could make out half of the van and the back of it.

His perspective was distorted by the thin glass, but he could still make out Veronica and Mandy's silhouettes, both hooded now, as they were led from the vehicle and down the alley. Drake could see the driver of the van, the two men in the back, and two others standing on either side of a red door at the end of the alley. They were wearing heavy overcoats, which, given the weather, someone only wore if they were hiding something beneath.

The men from the van handed the girls off and after a series of exchanges, they were ushered inside the building. A moment later, the two men reappeared at their posts at the door. They looked like Eastern Block fuckers, with huge shoulders and square heads, and Drake was having a hard time figuring out a way by them without getting his ass shot.

The waiter, a bald Chinese man came over to take his order. Drake initially only asked for a beer, but then an idea occurred to him.

"Soup," he said quickly.

"What kind of soup, Sir? We have over fourteen—"

Drake didn't take his eyes off the van.

"Any kind; spicy, real spicy. And I need it quick."

In his periphery, he saw the waiter frown and walk away.

In the alley, the driver with the gold incisor went back to the front seat of the van, while the other two climbed in the back. Drake was hoping that they would drive off, maybe go collect some other girls, but they seemed quite content in just sitting there.

"Please, just leave," he whispered.

"But I bring your beer," the waiter said, plunking a beer down on the table.

Drake shook his head.

"No, not you. Bring the soup as quick as you can."

Another frown, but the man left him alone.

Drake chugged half the beer, tilted it to one side, and then retained the rest for later.

As he waited for his soup, Drake debated his options. They were limited, to say the least. He could go around the other side of the building or maybe go through the Chinese restaurant to see if there was a passageway from this building to the next.

But something told him that Ken Smith and his comrades wouldn't be so stupid as to overlook something like that.

The other option was to try to get on the roof, but this seemed equally as implausible and would take too long. Veronica and Mandy had already been inside for five minutes.

God only knew what could happen to them in that time.

Drake's eyes drifted down to his beer. There was only one option left.

He sighed and reached into the pocket of his worn tartan sports coat and pulled out his mickey of Scotch.

He waited for the waiter to return with his soup, a giant steaming bowl that made Drake's eyes water even from three feet away, before he sipped his Scotch.

"No, no, no," the man said, shaking his head back and forth. "No alcohol—you must buy from me!"

Sorry about this, buddy.

"Fuck you," Drake slurred.

Then he took another swig.

The waiter placed the bowl down on the table and reached for the bottle of Scotch. Drake pulled away and drank some more. As he did, he swept his elbow across the table, knocking the beer bottle onto his lap.

Drake leaped to his feet.

"You spilled beer all over me!" He yelled. "What the fuck?"

He had to give the Chinese waiter credit. Even though the guy was about a buck ten soaking wet, he didn't back down from an apparent drunk who was at least twice his size.

"Get out!" the man screamed.

"You get out!" Drake shot back, sipping his mickey again.

"No, you get out! Get out or I call the police on you!"

Yeah, and I bet they'd take their sweet ass time coming down here. If they ever showed up, that is.

Drake took a deep breath and then took an aggressive step toward the waiter. As he did, he deliberately brought his knee up and banged the underside of the table.

Whereas the beer had been cold on his crotch, the soup was scalding.

The waiter's eyes went wide.

"Now you spilled the soup on me!" Drake shouted.

The waiter shook his head again and followed Drake as he staggered toward the door.

"You did! You spill everything!"

Drake, aware that his stomach was probably scalded from the soup and that he reeked like a Taiwanese fishing barge, took another swig of Scotch.

Then he opened the door and stepped into the night, shouting loud enough for everybody in the vicinity to overhear.

"Fuck you! You spilled shit all over me!"

The waiter followed him halfway out the door.

"Get out of here, you fucking drunk!" he screamed, and Drake couldn't help but smile.

Chapter 48

"LET ME OUT OF here!" Veronica screamed. She hammered on the glass and this time it seemed to flex a little. Or maybe it didn't; she couldn't be sure. "Let me the fuck out of here!"

The charade was over; she was veritably terrified now. For her, and for Mandy, wherever she was.

A booming voice suddenly filled the room.

"Step away from the glass," it instructed. Veronica turned her gaze upward and caught sight of a small intercom beside the red bulb.

"Fuck you!" she shouted back.

When there was no response, she went back to smacking the glass with open palms.

"Step away from the glass," the voice repeated.

This only encouraged her to bang harder.

"Step away from the glass," the voice ordered a third time. Only this time, it was accompanied by the sound of a small motor turning on.

Unlike the intercom, this time she couldn't find the source. That is until she heard a familiar crackle.

Pain shot up her left calf and caused her entire body to vibrate, from her toes to her molars. She yelped and jumped away from the wall, just in time to see what looked like a cattle prod retreating into the small hole in the Plexiglas.

Instead of moving away again, Veronica lunged for the hole, trying to grab either the opening or the cattle prod and yank it free.

But she was too slow, and the opening closed before she could grab anything.

She swore loudly and then stood in the middle of the room, her hands up.

"I'm away from the fucking glass," she shouted. "You happy now?"

The light above her blinked once.

"Oh, so we don't speak anymore? Now we're doing some sort of Morse code? One blink for yes, two for no? Is that it?"

Silence fell over the room, one so deep that she could hear her own heart beating in her ears.

She stood completely still, unsure of what to do next.

"Now what?" she said at last.

The voice that replied surprised her. It was loud like the previous one, but this time it had an accent that she couldn't quite place. It was a different person.

"Turn around and bend over."

Veronica almost laughed.

"Why don't you come in here and bend over," she yelled back. "Then I'll show you where to stick that cattle prod."

Even before Veronica finished the sentence, however, she heard the whirring sound again. Only, instead of coming from in front of her this time, it came from behind. Veronica smirked and moved away from the hole as another cattle prod extended toward her. The room was small, but it was large enough that whoever was holding the prod had to stick their entire arm in to zap her this time. And when it did, she was prepared to tear it from the socket.

"Come on, come on," she muttered. The cattle prod continued to extend, but when only six inches of it were in the room, it suddenly stopped.

Veronica didn't even see what happened next.

There was another blinding flash of pain, this time originating just below her right butt cheek, which sent her into convulsions.

The first zap had been painful, but this one was sheer agony. She didn't even see the prod, but knew that it must have come from behind her.

She screamed and her back arched. She almost collapsed when the prod unexpectedly retracted.

Somewhere in the back of her mind, she recognized that the red light had blinked twice during this attack.

"Turn around and bend over," the second voice repeated.

Veronica clenched her jaw and reluctantly obeyed.

"Now spread your ass cheeks," another voice, this one with a neutral accent, demanded.

Veronica shook her head. She wasn't squeamish, but this exploitation was too much even for her.

"No, I won't, no matter how many times—"

She heard the whir again and this time she saw four small squares in the Plexiglass open, one on each wall, all filled with the blinding light of a cattle prod. The first touched her ankle and she screamed, but still managed to stay upright. But when the second stung her left ass cheek, she collapsed to the ground in convulsions.

Veronica's face was suddenly wet with tears.

Where are you, Drake?

The red light above blinked three times, followed by a short pause and then another blink.

"Okay," she sobbed. "Okay, I'll do it."

When she finally coerced her trembling body to rise, she did as the voice demanded. Only then did she realize that the blinking light wasn't Morse code. They were bids. And now that she'd spread her ass cheeks, the light blinked six or seven times in rapid succession.

The auction, it appeared, had already begun.

Chapter 49

"FUCK YOU, TOO," DRAKE said as he stumbled toward the alley. As he crossed in front of the van, he finished the mickey and then tossed it. It struck the bumper and exploded in a shower of glass.

As expected, the driver started out the door with a sneer on his face.

"Get the fuck out of here, you bum," the Russian said, half in and half out of the van.

Drake gave him the finger and told him to fuck off.

"You say one more word..."

Drake stumbled toward the half-open door, his movements so uncoordinated that they almost set him off balance for real.

"Yeah, and what are you going to do?"

From the back of the van, someone barked something in Russian.

"Is just a fucking drunk. If he comes any closer, I'll knock his teeth down his throat," the driver hollered back.

"Oh, yeah?" Drake said. "I bet you couldn't even knock out your mother's dentures."

The Russian, who had been smirking up to this point, suddenly went deadpan.

"You fucking—"

Drake charged.

His act had been so compelling that the Russian never even saw it coming.

Drake's shoulder collided with the half-open door, catching the man partway out. The door crushed his midsection, knocking the wind out of him.

Before the Russian could recover, Drake yanked the door wide and the man slipped to the ground with a grunt. Then he reached inside his coat and pulled out his pistol. In a blink, he smashed the butt against the man's temple. His eyes rolled back in his head and he went limp.

Two more barks in Russian from behind him set Drake moving again.

He jumped into the van and smiled when he realized that it was still running. Then he jammed it into reverse and gunned it.

Glancing in the rearview, he saw that one of the men in the back was trying to get out, but got smoked by the open van door. Drake was lifted nearly a foot off the ground as the tires ran over his body. The second man had been leaning forward when Drake started to drive and was flung between the two front seats.

He tried to get up, but with his free hand, Drake grabbed the back of his head and forced it into the open ashtray. The man struggled to breathe, sending puffs of grey smoke and ash into the air.

The two men who had been standing guard by the red door tried to get out of the way, but there simply wasn't enough room. A moment before Drake felt that crunch of the van striking the brick wall, he released his grip on the back of the Russian's head. The man almost flew out of the back of the van, but his head cracked off the sidewall and he went still.

Drake immediately followed him, stepping over his limp body and examining the two guards at the door.

One was pinned between the bumper and the only part of the brick wall that had failed to blow inward, the other lay motionless on the ground, his head resting almost comfortably on the bed of the van. Drake looked at the only man who was still conscious, and then reached inside the Russian's jacket and pulled out the gun that was tucked beneath his thick overcoat.

The man's eyes went wide and he said something in Russian that Drake didn't understand.

It didn't matter.

Instead of shooting him, Drake just leaned over and slapped him gently across the face.

"How do you like my parking job?" he asked before leaping through the brick wall, the Russian's Tokarev pistol in one hand, his trusty 9mm in the other.

Chapter 50

VERONICA TRIED HER BEST to stay strong; she'd seen everything, she'd done everything, she's been a part of everything.

Or so she'd thought.

But this... being imprisoned in a glass box and forced to show off every square inch of her body, she felt worse than a piece of meat. She felt inorganic.

Veronica didn't want to give the bidders the satisfaction of seeing her cry, but she couldn't help it. It was the sheer helplessness of the situation, and she realized that this must not have been that different from what the girls must have felt in the shipping container.

She cried for them, too.

"Sit on the—"

Veronica, her face soggy with tears, looked upwards. This was the first time that any of the two dozen requests had stopped mid-sentence.

Not only that, but she felt a small tremor in the earth.

Worried that the cattle prods would come out again, Veronica made herself small in the center of the room.

But the command didn't continue. And the light, which had been blinking as frequently as a strobe in any of the strip clubs that she'd started out in, had also stopped.

Unsure of what was happening, Veronica remained as still as possible.

A minute passed, then two. After that, time was difficult to measure; the booth was completely soundproof, and all of her senses had been muted by the shock treatment.

When time stretched on and no further requests came, Veronica started to regain some of her former self.

Testing the waters, she slowly stood to her full height.

No more small doors opening, no cattle prods extending.

No commands from the speaker above, no blinking light.

Even though Veronica was hesitant to get her hopes up, a refrain began repeating in the back of her mind.

Drake's here… Drake's here… Drake's here… Drake's here…

Chapter 51

NO SOONER HAD DRAKE entered the hallway than two men came rushing toward him. Their faces were masks of confusion; for all they knew, he was just a man down on his luck trying to make a dollar delivering spicy Szechuan.

Drake went with this idea, putting the two guns behind his back.

"Hey! What's going on?" the closest man demanded. "Where's Ivan?"

"Special delivery," Drake quipped.

"What the—"

Drake swung his arm out and pistol whipped him in the jaw. There was an audible 'clack' and several of his teeth shot out of his mouth moments before he collapsed in a heap.

His partner, a stocky-looking man with tattoos that covered his bare arms, gaped at Drake. Then he started to pull a gun from his belt, but it got caught on something and Drake got the jump. He squeezed off two quick rounds from his own pistol. The first missed, sending shards of plaster into the air, but the other hit him directly on his left kneecap. The man screamed something in Russian, then dropped his gun to grab hold of his leg with both hands. Drake strode up to him, kicked him first in his wounded leg, which sent him falling backward, then delivered another to the side of his head.

His own pain from the exertion was mounting now, and Drake found himself bending awkwardly to one side as he searched the hallway for a door.

He found one just inside the opening he'd made in the wall with the van, but it required a keycard. Hearing more commotion heading his way, Drake tucked his pistol in the front of his jeans and tried the door handle.

It wouldn't even move in his hand.

He cursed then continued down the hallway until he made it to a fork. He glanced left, noted the doorway at the end of this hall, and then looked right.

And that's when he saw the bastard from the hangar. Their eyes locked for a moment, and recognition crossed over the short man's weathered face. Drake remembered the way he'd smirked, a cigarette dangling from his lips, his hand clutching a body bag containing one of the dead Colombian girls.

He wasn't smiling now.

Drake was surprised, however, that the man was still standing considering he had taken a bullet in the hip less than two days ago.

"Let's see you walk away from this," Drake said, raising the Tokarev pistol in his hand.

He fired three shots but wasn't prepared for the increased kick of the Russian handgun compared to his nine-millimeter: all three bullets missed.

Despite his injury, the man turned and bolted.

Drake's own internal turmoil was catching up with him, as well. He hurried after the Russian, but he was well aware that his pace had slowed and that the right side of his body was no longer in sync with the left.

And yet he pressed on.

Drake fired two more shots, one that embedded itself in the plaster above the man's head, while the other hit him in the shoulder. The force of the impact was enough to send him reeling forward.

Drake sprinted wanting to take advantage of the twice-wounded man, but the Russian still had one more surprise up his sleeve. He unfurled as Drake approached, revealing a Tokarev of his own.

"Fuck!"

Drake lunged to his left as the man fired three rounds.

Like Drake's first attempts, all three of the Russian's shots missed as well.

But they had come close; *too* close. Drake felt one whiz by his ear, and his hair was filled with plaster from the other two that were embedded just above the top of his head.

The sound was deafening in the hallway and Drake was momentarily disoriented. Thinking that he only had another second or two before the Russian took aim again, he forced himself off the wall, bringing the Tokarev up in front of his face.

But the Russian had other ideas. He pulled a keycard from his belt and unlocked the door at the end of the hall.

Not again, Drake thought as the man slipped through. He ran for the opening, leading with the handgun; it closed on the barrel.

Instinct had taken over now, and Drake's next actions barely registered in his brain. With his free hand, he grabbed the handle and pulled the door open, while at the same time shielding himself behind it.

Several more shots rang out, but all they did was pepper the hallway.

It was no longer just him and the squat Russian, Drake realized; he could hear shouts in different languages, with different accents coming from within the room.

It's now or never…

He swung around the open door, leading with the Tokarev. His body wanted to empty the clip into the dark interior, but his mind convinced him otherwise.

There could be girls in here. Mandy and Veronica could be in here.

Drake pressed his back against the wall while he waited for his eyes to adjust.

Two more bullets erupted from the darkness, one of which tore the sleeve of his sports coat. Drake immediately dropped into a crouch and tried to ascertain from which direction they'd come from.

Only he was momentarily taken aback by what he saw.

The interior of the hexagonal-shaped room reminded him of a Las Vegas sports book. Only, instead of having the screens on one wall and chairs situated across from it, the TVs were arranged in the center. Surrounding them were booths made of some sort of semitransparent glass that ran floor to ceiling like boxed-in cubicles. Inside of each, he could make out the outline of a figure.

His first thought was that these were the girls, but when the outline in the cubicle nearest him rose and started to bang on the glass, he knew differently.

These weren't the auction items, they were the buyers. And they appeared to be locked in their bidding rooms.

Drake scowled and he considered filling the man with bullets from the Tokarev.

And he might have, too, if it wasn't for another shot that struck the wall to his left.

This time, Drake saw where it had come from. He realized that behind the bidder booths was a narrow track that followed the circumference of the room. And while the Russian had gone right after entering, he'd gone all the way around and was now on Drake's left.

Drake emptied the Tokarev clip in the Russian's direction. Several of the bullets struck the booths, but instead of shattering the glass, they made softball-sized rosettes.

The shouts from the bidders intensified, and it took Drake a moment to figure out that they were coming from speakers embedded somewhere in the ceiling.

But he didn't give a shit about them; they could suffocate in there for all he cared.

What bothered Drake was that he could no longer see the Russian.

He tossed the spent Tokarev to the ground and pulled out his pistol. Then he started after the man, knowing that he was probably getting himself into a deadly ring around the rosy type, but no longer caring.

He was infuriated by the idea of this auction, by what had happened to those poor Colombian girls in the container. He was enraged for Veronica and Mandy and everyone else who preceded them.

"You better run! You better run, you asshole!" he shouted.

There was a tinkling sound from his right and he whipped the pistol around, his finger tensing on the trigger.

At the last second, he lowered the gun.

"Jesus Christ!" he shouted. "What are you doing in here? Run! *Run!*"

Chapter 52

"DRAKE!" VERONICA SHOUTED AS she hammered on the glass. *"Drake!"*

Despite the booth's soundproofing, she could hear loud bangs coming from somewhere nearby and even thought she could make out some voices.

Veronica couldn't tell what they were saying, but her mind filled in the blanks.

It was Drake; it had to be him and he was yelling her name, trying to find her. Her and Mandy.

To get them out of this fucking mess.

Veronica took a deep breath and then started pounding her fists on the glass with renewed vigor.

"Drake! In here! *I'm in here*!"

Chapter 53

IT WAS JUST A cocktail waitress.

The woman who had rushed toward Drake was a cocktail waitress of all things. Wearing only her bra and underwear, she was still unbelievably holding a tray of drinks in one hand.

And Drake had nearly blown her away.

He grabbed the waitress and shoved her behind him, the tray crashing loudly to the ground. Then he swept his gun from side to side. It was impossible for Drake to cover the waitress and both sides at once; all the Russian had to do was sneak up from the side he wasn't looking and with just a few bullets it would be game over for the both of them.

If only I could see through to the other side…

Drake focused his eyes on the monitors in the center of the hexagon, trying to catch a glimpse of the Russian.

But as he searched for the man, he found his gaze drawn to the monitors themselves.

And his heart sunk.

All of the screens that Drake could see showed the same thing: a naked woman standing in a room not unlike the bidder booths, bathed in a red glow. And in a strange irony, both the woman on screen and the bidders were all banging on the glass, begging to be released.

As haunting as this image was, it wasn't so much what the naked woman was doing, as it was the desperation in her tear-streaked features that disturbed Drake most.

"Veronica," he whispered. And then he started shouting. "Veronica! Veronica, I'm coming!"

Drake desperately wanted to put a third bullet in the Russian bastard, but his vengeance would have to wait. He also wished to take out every last one of the sick bastards bidding for Veronica's life.

But he had a better idea.

"Where is that room?" Drake shouted over his shoulder at the now whimpering cocktail waitress.

"*No entiendo*!" she screamed back.

Drake cursed himself for not paying attention in Spanish class and then gestured with his free hand for her to move toward the door that he'd entered.

"Open it! Open it!" he instructed.

There was a pause and Drake turned to look at the waitress to make sure that she understood. Evidently, she did, as the keypad beeped and turned green, but with his head turned, Drake didn't see the Russian approach.

He heard the shots, though, and felt a sear of pain shoot up his right calf.

Drake whipped around and fired blindly into the darkness, but his bullets only embedded in the bulletproof glass.

The Russian was gone again.

Gritting his teeth against the pain, Drake backed out the door, following after the waitress.

Once in the hallway, he slammed the door closed behind them.

"*Te dispararon*," the waitress said, her wide eyes drifting to his right calf.

"No shit," Drake grumbled, but he didn't have time to assess his wound. Because he'd managed to hobble out of the viewing room, it couldn't be too serious.

Or maybe it was.

In the end, it didn't matter. What mattered was getting Veronica and Mandy out of this hell hole.

He gestured for the woman to back up and then squeezed off a single round.

The keypad beside the door exploded in a shower of sparks and Drake heard a deadbolt automatically slide into place. Just to make sure, he grabbed the handle and pulled.

It didn't budge.

"I hope you all suffocate in there," he whispered.

Satisfied that neither the Russian bastard nor the auction bidders would be able to get out, Drake turned back to the waitress.

"The woman in the box with the red light," he said, trying to speak as clearly as possible. "Do you know where she is? Do you know how I can find her?"

The waitress shrugged and shook her head, but Drake didn't know if this was because she didn't understand or because she didn't know where Veronica was.

"Okay, okay, you run," he said, pointing down the long hallway that led to the busted brick wall.

This, the waitress appeared to understand. As she turned, Drake reached out and snatched the keycard that dangled from her hip. The waitress didn't seem to notice; she was already sprinting down the hallway.

"Run! *Rápido! Rápido!*"

Drake, his leg now soaked with blood as well as beer and spicy Asian soup, hobbled after her, but instead of making his way toward the van still embedded in the brick wall, he continued straight.

There was a single door at the end of this hallway, and he knew that that was where Veronica must be held.

Gritting his teeth against the agony in his side and leg, Drake scanned the waitress's card on the keypad and pulled the door wide, leading with his pistol.

Chapter 54

THE FIRST THING THAT Drake saw was the girl, only it wasn't Veronica.

She was nude, sitting on the edge of the bed with her back to the door. And yet, Drake thought he recognized her long blond hair.

"Mandy?"

The woman turned, and he realized that it was indeed Mandy.

The second thing Drake saw was the man sitting on the bed beside her. Like Mandy, his back was also facing the door.

But it was what was on his back that gave Drake pause: a massive black and white tattoo that ran from between his shoulder blades to the small of his back. It was an incredibly detailed depiction of a Cobra with a photorealistic eyeball in its mouth. It was the symbol for ANGUIS Holdings and similar to the one that Raul had on his forearm and the one on the sign for the Church of Liberation in Colombia, all those years ago.

"Mandy," Drake repeated, and this time the man turned his head.

He had a thick black beard and shortly cropped hair that was graying at the temples. Even though Drake had never seen a picture of the man, he knew without a doubt who this person was.

It was Boris Brackovich.

There was something in his eyes and that, combined with the slight smirk on his lips that he shared with Ken Smith and everyone else who had *fuck you* money, that gave him away.

The tattoo was a fairly good indication, as well.

He was also the man responsible for all of this mess, for the sex auction, for the dead girls in the shipping container.

For Veronica being trapped in a glass box.

And while Drake recognized this man, it was clear that Boris also knew who he was.

"Damien Drake," he said in a voice that lacked any accent at all.

Drake aimed the gun directly at the center of Boris's back.

He felt like putting a bullet in the man then, putting an end to all of this. But that would be too easy.

And besides, it wasn't part of the plan.

Drake wanted Boris, but he wanted Ken Smith even more.

"Guilty," Drake said with a shrug. "Mandy, come over here."

As he spoke, Drake took the two pieces of his cell phone out of his pocket.

"Mandy, come over here," Drake repeated.

Boris might be tough, but if he could snap a few pictures of the man in this place, in a compromised situation, they would go a long way to getting him to flip on Ken Smith.

It would either be that or prison, and even men as well connected as Boris would have a difficult time surviving in Rikers, especially considering what he'd done to the girls.

Drake slipped the battery into his cell phone and it clicked into place. He waited for the screen to boot up.

"I know what you're thinking, Drake, because I was once like you. Naive, broke, at the whim of others. You think you can snap a few pictures and that'll be enough to put me away," Boris chuckled, a dry, irritating sound. "Drake, you could take pictures of me strangling this Colombian *shlyukha* and it wouldn't do shit. I'd get off and the best part? My lawyers would get you and all of the NYPD to issue a public apology. That's what having money means. It's pure, unadulterated *power*. Power to do what—"

Drake was only half listening when he caught movement out of the corner of his eye.

Mandy had a pair of scissors in her hand and she lunged at Boris.

"Mandy, no!"

She was aiming for his neck, but even though Boris had been focused on Drake, he managed to get his arm up in time. The scissors embedded in his triceps, but this didn't seem to faze him. Boris's other arm shot out with lightning speed and collided with the side of Mandy's head. She fell backward off the bed and landed with a loud *thunk.*

Drake grit his teeth and strode forward.

"I won't put you in prison, I'll put you in a pine box, you—"

But now it was his turn to be cut off.

Something smashed into the back of Drake's head, something big and hard. Something that sent stars across his vision.

Drake collapsed to one knee and then someone pressed down on the bullet hole in his right calf, and the stars vanished.

They were replaced by pure darkness.

Chapter 55

DRAKE COULDN'T HAVE BEEN out for more than a minute or two, but in that time, his assailant had somehow managed to place him in a chair and bind his hands behind his back.

His eyelids fluttered and it took several seconds for his vision to clear.

Boris was standing in front of him, fully dressed now, holding Drake's cell phone only inches from his face.

The man was smiling, a thin line of perfectly white teeth embedded in his dark beard.

"I guess we'll never find out if your pictures would do any good," Boris said, wagging the phone. "You fucked up, Drake. You didn't take any pictures, didn't even call the cops. My men will have this place cleaned up in under an hour. But you'll be long gone by then. Nothing you did today matters, Drake. Don't you get that? *None of it matters*. Tomorrow we'll open up a new shop, with new girls, and more buyers than you can imagine. This is only the start of our empire. The beginning. With what—"

Drake started to laugh. He hadn't intended to, but it just felt natural given the circumstances.

"Why are you laughing?" Boris demanded, his smile vanishing. Then he lifted his head to somebody hovering over Drake's left shoulder. "Why the fuck is he laughing?"

Drake craned his head to see who it was, who had knocked him out.

And then he laughed even harder.

"I should have known that you'd be here, you slimy bastard," he said between breaths.

Raul stepped out from behind him and crouched down low.

"We could have worked together, Drake. That's what Ken wanted. But now it has come to this. I'm afraid that your usefulness has run out—you and your brother."

This only made Drake laugh even harder. He laughed so hard that his face got hot and he felt himself on the verge of hyperventilating.

Boris backed away from Drake.

"Raul, why the fuck is he laughing? Why in God's name is he laughing?"

"Because—" Drake began, but couldn't get any more words out.

Raul leaned back and slapped Drake hard across the face. But the laughter didn't stop.

"Raul, what the fuck is going on here?"

Raul shook his head and said, "I dunno. But we should get out of here."

Boris grimaced.

"Because it's not—" but Drake broke down again before he could finish.

Raul leaned back again, but this time instead of slapping him, he placed his thumb directly on the bullet hole in his calf and pressed down.

Drake screamed in agony.

"Now are you going to tell us why you're laughing, Drake?"

Drake hissed through clenched teeth.

"Because," he finally managed. "This wasn't about pictures, you fucking idiots. This wasn't a photoshoot and I never intended to call the police." Drake's tone suddenly turned deadly serious. "I was relying on them to trace the phone that you're holding in your hand."

Boris's face went completely slack and he dropped the cell phone as if it was suddenly scalding. Even Raul, who had the emotional spectrum of a slug, seemed to become agitated.

"That's right, you fucking morons. Your buddy DI Palmer should be in here any minute. He's gonna bring the Sgt. with him and I'd like to see you explain this situation. So, yeah, you should run. You should run as fast as you can. Because I'm going to get you. You and that bastard Ken Smith. I'm not going to stop until everyone involved with ANGUIS Holdings is either dead or in jail. And that, Boris, is *true* power."

Chapter 56

"IT'S BACK ONLINE! IT'S back online!" Dunbar shouted. "Drake's cell phone is online!"

Sgt. Yasiv leaned over the back of the detective's seat as he punched away on the keyboard.

"Do you have a lock on it? Do you know where Drake is?"

"Working on it. It's somewhere in Hell's Kitchen, gimme a second," Dunbar replied, still hammering away at the keys.

Sgt. Yasiv lifted his head to the driver.

"Murray, drive!" he instructed. "Take us to Hell's Kitchen!"

The mobile command center lurched forward and Yasiv braced himself on the back of Dunbar's seat.

I hope you got out of there, Drake, Yasiv thought. *I hope to god that you had enough time to get the fuck out of there.*

"Got it!" Detective Dunbar exclaimed, leaning back from his computer. "It's on West 41st! West 41st and 11th Ave!"

The van immediately careened to the right.

"Hold on!" Officer Murray called back.

They veered around a corner and then Dunbar turned to look at Yasiv with wide eyes.

"Should I call him now? Should I call DI Palmer?"

Yasiv chewed the inside of his lip and then nodded.

If it were up to him, he'd hold out as long as possible before getting Palmer involved. But this was Drake's operation, not his.

And Drake wanted the Deputy Inspector to see this.

"Call DI Palmer and let him know we've found Drake."

"ETA Six minutes!" Murray hollered. "Hold on tight, it's gonna get dicey."

Yasiv gripped the back of Dunbar's seat.

I hope to God you got out of there, Drake.

Chapter 57

AS SOON AS THE pain in his calf subsided, Drake started laughing again. He laughed when Boris tripped over the bed as he scrambled toward the door. He laughed at the expression on Raul's previously unflappable face.

He laughed at the absurdity, the sheer lunacy of it all.

When he heard the muted sounds of sirens reach him from within the nearly soundproof room, he continued to laugh.

He pictured the auction bidders stuck in their stalls, waiting to be rescued.

Waiting to be *arrested*.

And this made him laugh even harder.

He hadn't gotten Ken, and both Raul and Boris were more than likely going to get away. But Boris was wrong. What he'd done here, what Drake and his friends had accomplished, *meant* something. They had put a serious wrench in Ken's plans. And people would take notice.

DI Palmer would have no choice but to let Sgt. Yasiv dig deep into the connections between Smith and Brackovich. The public pressure would be too great, the outrage at the idea of auctioning off human lives right here in New York would not go ignored.

Sure, it meant that Drake would likely be pining away in a prison cell somewhere for what he'd done to Officer Kramer, but it was worth it.

Eventually, he'd get out. And when he did, he'd continue his pursuit of Ken Smith and the other people behind ANGUIS Holdings.

The only thing that stopped Drake's chuckling was the sound of someone groaning.

Mandy pulled herself to her feet and massaged the side of her head. Other than a welt above her right eye, she looked no worse for wear.

Veronica was right, this girl had some stones. She *could* look after herself.

I just hope you're okay, too, V.

At first, when Mandy's eyes fell on Drake, confusion washed over her. But when she realized that they were alone in the room, that Raul and Boris were gone, she grabbed something off the dresser and hurried over to him.

"Are you okay?" she asked.

The back of his head throbbed from where Raul had struck him, but Drake didn't think that it was serious. He was more concerned about his leg; he could no longer feel anything below his right knee.

"I'll be fine," he said quietly. "You should get out of here."

Mandy took a step back and observed him for a moment.

"Drake, you're the one who needs to get out of here. The police are coming, and they're going to arrest you. They're going to arrest you for what I did out at the—"

Drake shook his head.

"*I* did that," he said. "I hit Kramer and locked him in the container. Go with Veronica, she'll take care of you. *Please.*"

Mandy bowed her head and walked behind Drake.

But she didn't go to the door. Instead, she cut him free of his bindings.

And then she leaned close to his ear.

"Thank you," Mandy said, before kissing him on the cheek.

Still confused by this sudden turn of events, Drake shook his head and then groaned as he pulled himself to his feet.

"No, thank you, Mandy."

But Mandy was already gone.

The sirens were louder now and Drake knew he didn’t have much time. But with his leg the way it was, he didn’t know if he was going to make it out of there before the cops arrived.

But Drake wasn’t one for quitting.

Chapter 58

SGT. HENRY YASIV STARED in amazement at the parade of men that were brought handcuffed out of the auction. He counted at least eleven of them, eleven well-dressed men sporting everything from pinstripe suits to a sultan's robes.

He could barely contain his disgust. His first instinct after they'd blown through the door to the auction room was to leave again, to let them rot in there.

But now, seeing them hang their heads in shame as they were led out of the place, he felt a modicum of satisfaction. But it didn't last long.

"He's not here!" somebody shouted. Yasiv turned in the direction of the voice. "Drake's not fucking here!"

Yasiv felt his anger bubble over as he stared at DI Palmer. The man was notorious for keeping his cool, but now that the trace had only revealed Drake's phone and not the man himself, Palmer was irate.

With Yasiv watching on, Palmer grabbed a uniformed officer by the collar and screamed in his face, demanding to know where Drake was. The young cop was so startled that he could barely produce a full sentence.

Yasiv grabbed DI Palmer's arm, and the man let go of the officer and spun around.

"You knew that he wasn't going to be here!" Palmer accused. "You knew it, didn't you?"

Yasiv said nothing, but couldn't help the smirk that crossed his lips.

DI Palmer leveled a finger directly at his nose.

"If I find out you've had something to do with this, that you helped him get away, I swear to God, Yasiv, you won't just be out of a job, but you'll be locked away."

Yasiv felt oddly calm in the face of such anger and remained mum.

But inside, he was begging for Palmer to strike him. With all of these other officers and detectives milling about, there was no way that Palmer could talk his way out of that one. Not even Ken Smith would be able to help him.

"Let me go!" a female voice shouted, drawing both Palmer's and Yasiv's attention.

A petite woman with blond hair was thrashing in the arms of a police officer, struggling to free herself. She was wearing a strange nightgown that seemed two sizes too big for her.

Yasiv squinted. The woman seemed familiar and the last time he'd seen her she'd also been wearing a nightgown… only that one had been too small, not too big.

And it had been adorned with Anna from Frozen.

What the hell is she *doing here?*

"Let her go," Sgt. Yasiv ordered.

The officer holding her raised an eyebrow.

"Sorry?"

"You heard me: let her go," Yasiv repeated.

Out of the corner of his eye, Yasiv spotted an officer making his way not toward the scene as most others were, but away from it. He was wearing an NYPD police hat, but the rest of the uniform didn't match—he was wearing plainclothes. And despite the fact that he was walking with a limp, there was something about his gait that Yasiv recognized.

"And that's my purse! Give me my fucking purse!" the woman demanded.

This new officer, like the first, turned to Sgt. Yasiv for advice. It was strange how these trained policemen could deal with the likes of Russian mobsters, drug dealers, and biker gangs, but when they were confronted by a feisty woman, they had no idea how to act.

"Give her her purse back, Jesus," Sgt. Yasiv said with a sigh. The officer obliged, and Yasiv turned back to the strange man with the limp.

DI Palmer must have followed his gaze, because he suddenly spoke up.

"Where the hell do you think you're going?

But the officer didn't turn; instead, he ducked his head low and hobbled even more quickly away from the scene.

Palmer took a step toward the man.

"I'm talking to you! Hey, officer! Don't you walk away from me."

Yasiv's eyes flicked back to the woman who had since gotten her purse and they exchanged a knowing glance. The woman's wide eyes then darted three times over to the man whom Palmer was addressing.

And that's when Yasiv finally understood; he knew where he'd seen this woman before, and he knew who the man with the limp was.

He reached for Palmer's arm and tried to turn him around, but the DI just shook him off.

"You fucking *asshole*!" Veronica suddenly shouted. "You bastard!"

Yasiv looked back in time to see a squat Russian man with gray hair being dragged in handcuffs through the hole in the wall. He was snarling and barking something in Russian to the two police officers who held him. As he watched, Veronica reached into her purse and pulled out a Taser.

Oh, shit.

"Fuck you!" Veronica screamed as she ran at the man.

There was a crackle as she drove the Taser into the man's midsection. Yasiv saw his eyes roll back and his body tense. But Veronica wasn't done yet. She pulled the Taser back, only to thrust it forward again, this time aiming for the man's crotch.

The noise of the Taser and the shriek that followed was so loud that it drew nearly everyone's attention.

Yasiv started toward the woman, anticipating that Palmer would follow.

And he did.

When they reached Veronica, it took both of them to pull her off the Russian man who had since started to drool.

Yasiv relaxed and Veronica broke free. This time, she kicked the man in the crotch.

"That's for Nancy!" she kicked again. "That's for Mandy! And this one…" she reared back and delivered a kick so vicious that the man's knees buckled and he collapsed to the ground, nearly taking the two officers down with him. "And that's for me, you piece of shit."

Veronica held her hands up and stepped back.

Grinning now, Yasiv looked over his shoulder for the plainclothed officer in the hat, but he couldn't find him anywhere.

Yasiv's grin became a full-fledged smile.

Drake was gone.

Chapter 59

"**HURRY! WE NEED TO** get the fuck out of here!" Boris shouted at Raul as they sprinted down the hallway.

Carnage was all around them; his men were lying on the floor moaning, blood leaking from various wounds.

One person did this?

But when he saw the van halfway inside the goddamn building, he shook his head.

Impossible.

Boris managed to slide through the opening and then squeezed himself between the brick wall and the side of the cargo van.

As he moved, the sirens got louder. They were coming from the east, so when he cleared the alley, he pointed in that direction.

"Raul, you run that way! Go find Ken… tell him what happened here. Tell him what Drake did!"

The impish man stared at Boris for a moment and for a split second he thought that Raul would ignore his request. But without saying a word, the man started running east.

Boris hurried the other way, passing in front of a Chinese restaurant. People were staring at him, he realized, and it was mostly due to the fact that he was wearing a button-down shirt and suit pants.

I need to change; I need to change, find a car, and get the fuck out here.

Resisting the urge to run and draw more attention to himself, Boris walked briskly toward the next alley. He slid into the shadows, thankful to no longer be out in the open.

Halfway to the conjoining street, he spotted a bum curled up beneath an over-sized NYU sweatshirt.

The idea of wearing the sweatshirt made him cringe—God only knew what it was infested with—but he had no choice.

People had seen him leave the auction, they'd seen him in his button-down and suit bottoms.

Heart racing, Boris reached down and yanked the sweatshirt off the bum.

He felt resistance as he started to walk away, and he shot a leg out without even bothering to look where he kicked.

"Fuck off," he snapped.

He'd just managed to put his head and one arm through when the bum spoke and he stopped cold.

"Boris? Boris Brackovich? Is that really you?"

Boris, eyes wide, turned to face the voice.

It had come from the bum, only the man wasn't a bum anymore—probably never was.

It was a handsome man with short, bleached-blond hair.

And he was smiling.

"You've been a bad boy, Boris. And now it's time to pay."

When Boris saw the glint of the blade in the man's hand, it was already too late.

All he could do was scream.

***

Beckett used the NYU sweatshirt to clean the blood off his hands as he made his way back to his car.

There were sirens all around him now, but this time he wasn't going to hang around. He needed to get out of there and fast.

Parked just one block over, Beckett made it to his car without being spotted. Two squad cars had driven by, their sirens blazing, but they paid him no heed.

He balled up the sweatshirt and took his keys out of his pocket to unlock the trunk. Only when he got closer, he realized that it was slightly ajar.

His heart started to thud in his chest even harder than it had when he'd killed Boris Brackovich.

With trembling fingers, Beckett opened the trunk.

"No," he moaned. *"No."*

It was gone; the bag of bloody clothes and balaclava from Bob Bumacher's house were missing.

Beckett heard a grunt from behind him and whipped around, slipping the scalpel blade from beneath the sweatshirt.

It appeared to be a police officer, but he was in rough shape. The man was shuffling along, his left shoulder rubbing up against the buildings as he moved at a snail's pace.

Beckett swallowed hard and his eyes flicked down to the blade in his hand.

Did he see me? Do I have to… could I even…

But then the man lifted his head and peered at Beckett from beneath the brim of his NYPD hat.

Beckett gasped, then tossed both the sweatshirt and scalpel into the trunk and slammed it closed. Then he ran over to the man and wrapped his arm around his waist.

"It looks like you could use a ride, Drake. Come on, let's get the fuck out of here."

Epilogue

TWO MONTHS LATER

ALL EYES WERE ON the TV screen, including Sgt. Yasiv's. Deputy Inspector Lewis Palmer stood at the podium, his face pale, his eyes downcast. It was a recording of the first official news conference after the events that had transpired in Hell's Kitchen.

"First of all, myself and Mayor Smith would like to send our greatest admiration and congratulations to the hard-working men of the 62nd precinct, as well as the other precincts that helped solve one of the largest sex trafficking scandals in the history of New York. To date, we have indicted twenty-three individuals for crimes that vary from human trafficking, solicitation, unlawful and forceful confinement, among others. We also seized more than one hundred kilos of heroin in a related bust."

When DI Palmer paused to catch his breath, a woman in the audience spoke up.

"Can you tell us about Boris Brackovich's death?"

Palmer's brow furrowed.

"We can confirm that real estate magnate Boris Brackovich was found deceased in the vicinity of the crime scene."

"But can you confirm that he was involved in the sex auction?"

DI Palmer shook his head.

"At this time, all we know is that Boris was found dead with multiple stab wounds to his neck and chest. As the investigation is ongoing, we—"

"Are you telling me that that **bleep* *bleep* *bleep** Boris wasn't buying young Colombian girls so that he could **bleep* *bleep* *bleep** them?"

The string of profanities that followed was so lengthy that Sgt. Yasiv couldn't even make out the context of the sentence.

The camera panned to the audience and the woman who had been addressing Palmer appeared on screen.

"There," DI Palmer said, leaning forward. "Pause it right there."

He tapped the screen.

"That woman, she was there that night. She was the one who tased the Russian. I swear it."

Yasiv stared at the still image.

"It could be, but it's hard to tell. It was a crazy time and—"

Palmer shook his head.

"No, that's her. I know it. I know—"

Yasiv turned his back to the man and reached into his pocket. He pulled out a well-worn piece of paper and unfolded it.

ANGUIS Holdings, the title read. Below that were four names: Boris Brackovich, Steffani Loomis, Horatio Dupont, and Mendes Corporation. Boris's name had been crossed out.

At the bottom of the page, there was a fifth: Ken Smith.

"One down, four to go," Yasiv said under his breath.

An arm tugged on his sleeve and Yasiv quickly folded the paper and slid into his pocket.

"What's up?"

Detective Dunbar stared back, a frightened expression on his round face.

"Come with me," he said quickly. "I need to show you something"

Yasiv, his concern growing, followed Dunbar out of the room. The detective led him to his office and then indicated his computer screen.

Yasiv swallowed hard as he took a seat behind the desk.

Onscreen was a photocopy of a newspaper article written in Spanish. In the center, surrounded by text, was a full-color image of a burning boat. Even though the stern was partly obscured by flames, Yasiv saw enough to recognize the name: *B-Yacht'ch.*

"It gets worse," Dunbar whispered. He leaned over and clicked a few buttons and another image popped up.

Yasiv felt his chest implode.

It was another image of the boat from a different angle, but inlaid on this one was a black and white headshot of a person who looked nearly identical to Damien Drake.

Suddenly feeling dizzy, Yasiv reached into his pocket and pulled out a cheap flip phone.

"Should we tell him?" Dunbar asked, his eyes locked on the screen.

Yasiv nodded; he had already started to dial the number.

***

"Congratulations, you two are the proud parents of a beautiful baby boy. Have you thought of a name?" the nurse said as she handed the bundle of screaming child over to Jasmine.

Drake stared at the baby, his eyes brimming with tears. Then he looked at Jasmine and saw that she was crying, too.

They hadn't discussed the name, but when their eyes met, something unspoken passed between them.

"Clay," Jasmine said softly, and Drake found himself nodding. "I think we're going to call him Clay."

The nurse rested a hand on Jasmine's shoulder and offered her a smile.

"I think that's a great name," she said. "I'll leave you two alone. If you need anything, just press the red button by your head."

"Can you tell Suzan to come in here, please?" Drake asked, and the nurse nodded.

"You know, I wish you'd shave that beard off your face. Can you imagine that being the first thing you see of your dad? A ratty, salt-and-pepper beard?" Jasmine said as she pressed the child against her bare chest.

Drake chuckled and wiped more tears from his eyes.

Jasmine's expression softened.

"You want to hold him?"

Drake couldn't remember the last time he'd held a baby.

"Where's Suzan? She should be in here."

"Don't worry about her, she'll be back—probably just went for a coffee. Here, hold your son, Drake."

He reached for Clay, but as he did, something in his pocket vibrated.

Jasmine's brow furrowed.

"What is it?"

Drake pulled the burner phone out of his pocket and stared at it before answering. There were only a handful people who had the number, and since he'd gotten it about two months ago it had never rung.

Swallowing hard, Drake stepped away from the hospital bed and answered the phone.

"Drake, it's Yasiv. I'm afraid… I'm afraid something happened to your brother."

Drake listened carefully to what the man had to say, but even before Yasiv was done speaking, the phone slipped from his hand and crashed to the floor.

"What's wrong? Drake, what's wrong?" Jasmine asked, concern in her voice.

Drake could barely speak his throat was so constricted.

"It's my brother… I think I have to go… I think I have to go to Colombia."

Jasmine's eyes went wide.

"Now? What—"

There was a commotion outside the door a second before it burst open.

"You can't go in there!" Suzan Cuthbert exclaimed.

"I can do whatever I want," a familiar voice said.

Drake turned and looked at DI Palmer as the man approached, a beaming smile plastered on his face.

There was nothing Drake could do. He had nowhere left to hide, nowhere to run.

"I knew that if I followed Suzan for long enough, she'd lead me to you," he said.

Suzan swore and reached for Palmer, but one of the uniformed officers that followed the DI into the room grabbed her.

"I wouldn't make any vacation plans just yet," Palmer continued as he hooked a handcuff around one of Drake's wrists, and the other to the chair. "You have a pending date with a 4 x 6 first."

"Leave him alone!" Jasmine shouted. Clay started to cry and the nurse suddenly appeared out of nowhere. She scooped up the child and held it protectively against her bosom. "Why can't you just leave us alone?"

DI Palmer raised an eyebrow and stared at Jasmine.

"Leave you alone? No, I'm sorry, not when you and I are just becoming acquainted. I'm thinking that you might want to start looking for a babysitter, though. If you want some recommendations, I'd be happy to help."

"Get out of here!" Jasmine screamed. "Get the hell out of here!"

Drake finally realized what was happening and he felt his heart drop into the pit of his stomach.

"No!"

DI Palmer nodded.

"Yes, Drake, yes," then, as he slapped a new set of handcuffs on Jasmine, Palmer leaned in close and whispered in Drake's ear. "Ken told you not to fuck with him, so did Raul. This is your fault, Drake. Everyone would've been better off if you just stayed dead at the Reynolds's farm."

The End

Author's Note

I'll be the first to admit it: when I first started writing about Damien Drake a little over a year ago, I knew very little about him. I knew that he had a troubled past, likes his Scotch, and really, really wants to do good.

But that's about it.

Now, five books in, I know more about Drake than nearly any of the other characters I have ever written about. He still tries his best to do what he thinks is right, but more often than not, he stumbles. I think that his friends, the few that he still has anyway, recognize this in him, which is why they continue to put up with his shit.

That being said, I don't have a clue how Drake will be as a father or how the hell he's going to get out of his current jam.

But that's the fun, isn't it? Just as the excitement for you, dear reader, is at least partly derived from the mystery of what's going to happen next, I have a similar experience in writing the books.

I learn along with the characters, share in their adventures, their fears, their pain, and their pleasure. Maybe not as viscerally as them, but...

And this makes my job as a writer the best job ever. Creativity is a uniquely human endeavor, one that feeds the spirit and nurtures the soul. The fact that I can write books and make a living doing it is something that I often marvel at. And I have you to thank for that.

So, you want to know what happens to Drake next? Welcome to the club. Look for *DRUG LORD: PART I,* due out at the end of August.

And, finally, here comes the annoying part when I ask you for a review. Look, I get it, you're busy reading books. But if you have a spare moment, direct your browser to Amazon and leave a review for HUMAN TRAFFIC.

If you do, I might just let Drake live 😊.

You keep reading, and I'll keep writing.

Best,
Patrick
Montreal, 2018

Made in the USA
Middletown, DE
16 September 2021